An *A Thieving Curse* Companion Novella

The Dragon Prince's Heart

Selina R. Gonzalez

NOTE:

This companion novella retells the beginning of *A Thieving Curse* from the perspective of the love interest, Alexander, and is best enjoyed after reading A Thieving Curse.

THE DRAGON PRINCE'S HEART: AN *A THIEVING CURSE* COMPANION NOVELLA
Copyright © 2021 by Selina R. Gonzalez.
All rights reserved.

Published by Wyvern Wing Press
www.WyvernWingPress.com
www.SelinaRGonzalez.com

The Dragon Prince's Heart

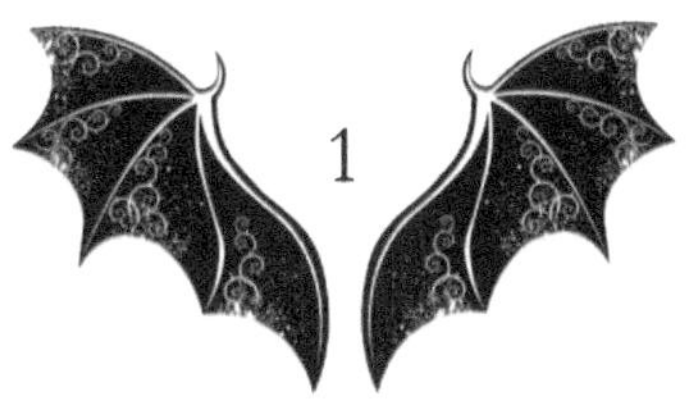

A strangled gasp stuck in Alex's throat as he bolted upright in the dark, his chest heaving. Something had tangled his wings so he couldn't move, couldn't escape.

With a growl, he lashed out, and his claws ripped through…

His blanket.

All at once, his mind caught up to his surroundings. The glowing embers in his fireplace provided a dim illumination to his looming closet and small bookshelf against the rough stone walls, but his dragon vision compensated for the darkness, casting everything in red-tinted light. His bed squeaked beneath him. Heat raged in his chest, but he forced himself to take deep breaths and quiet the dragon. He couldn't shift in this little cave.

Alex looked over the room again, and some of the tension in his shoulders eased.

He was alone. No lords accusing Alex of murdering his parents. No Henry sneering as he pushed a sword through his heart. No Lucas standing by and approving of the death of the monster.

As his breathing steadied, he tossed his legs over the side of the bed and rested his forearms on his knees. A book lay sprawled on the stone floor, and he picked it up with a sigh. He'd fallen asleep reading again, which wasn't surprising, since he'd been reading one of Jasper's treatises on kingship that always made him sleepy. To Alex, the book's primary usefulness was inducing sleep. He glanced at the dying fire. Unfortunately, falling asleep while reading explained why he'd forgotten to add enough logs to last the entire night, and the room had cooled more than he liked. Cold aggravated the dragon, and that made the nightmares worse.

Twelve years. Twelve years since his uncle cursed him, and he sometimes wondered if he'd ever stop having nightmares. Still… Alex thought for a moment, calculating how long it had been since the last one. Four months wasn't bad. Better than once a week. Or most nights, like they had been at nine.

His scale-covered tail wrapped around his waist as if it had a mind of its own and wanted to comfort him. He flicked it down with a scowl. The awkward thing and its traitorous penchant for exposing his emotions was his least favorite physical aspect of his curse.

His second least favorite aspect was the claws. He examined one of the new rips in his blanket with dismay. As he couldn't sew—the long, sharp claws had proven counterproductive to mending efforts— he'd either have to live with the holes, which would only get worse…or admit to Meredith what had happened. But he hated the way the others looked at him when he admitted to having another nightmare. Like he was fragile.

He chuckled ruefully. Alexander, the fragile, fire-breathing dragon.

There was little hope that he would fall asleep again, so he returned the book to the bookshelf, then pulled on his boots and headed out of the cave. He needed a distraction. Something to forget the nightmare of things that hadn't happened, but still felt real.

It was dark outside, the crescent moon high in the star-covered sky. At least that meant there were still several hours until dawn. Good. The dark would hide him, and he could fly without worrying about being seen.

A fiery pressure behind his sternum demanded Alex release the dragon, but he was too emotionally compromised to risk a shift. He unfurled his wings and took to the sky in his human form. Although it was more tiring, he preferred to keep as much control as possible, especially after a nightmare, so he rarely shifted to his full dragon form.

As he flew, the crisp scent of pines and earth and the gentle whistle of air past his horns soothed his senses. The nightmare melted away in the face of the freedom he found in the wide-open sky. Hazy tendrils of clouds drifted overhead, the stars in the heavens beyond shining down with a ruby tint due to his dragon vision. He could never stay in a bad mood long while flying. In the unending expanse over the mountains, his fears and problems seemed as small and inconsequential as the nocturnal animals he glimpsed scurrying between trees far below.

Even the cold of an early spring night wasn't enough to mute his enjoyment of the near-weightless sensation of soaring over the treetops. Winter was another matter altogether, and Lucas never could resist a friendly jab when Alexander sat in front of a roaring fire wrapped in a blanket after a trek through the snow.

A scream tore through the stillness, and Alex's wings seized. He came to himself just before crashing into the top of a towering pine tree. Had he imagined that? Some facet of his nightmare playing tricks on his waking mind?

"No!" Definitely a female's panicked shout, and not in his imagination. Alex strained his hearing and sniffed the air, his heart thumping in double time to the rhythm of his wings.

Blood. Faint, but there. He heard snarls and a human breathing hard. Someone needed help. This deep into the mountains, more than raccoons came out at night, and Alex knew from bitter experience he wasn't the only monster to be found near his cave on Mount Klainar. But if needed, he could be the largest.

He sped toward the sound of growls, his dragon eyes scanning the shadows below as he sailed low over the trees. Another sniff brought clearer scents. *Wolves. Human. Horse.*

A *crack* and another high-pitched scream assaulted his ears, and Alex stopped listening so closely with a wince. He darted between treetops, his cramped wings brushing against pine needles.

There.

Wolves surrounded a blonde girl. One canine gripped her cloak in its teeth, and another prepared to spring. The girl threw her hands in front of her face, and Alex let loose a desperate roar. Heat grew in his torso, but he swallowed the fire back so he wouldn't accidentally hurt the girl. The wolves whined and cowered, their snouts twitching as they caught the scent of smoke on his breath, then fled into the forest. Alex landed a few feet away from the girl, who was staring after the retreating beasts.

The tang of blood pricked at his nostrils, and the dragon reached for it, eager. Alex shoved down the sickening sensation as the girl finally pivoted toward him. He stepped forward and opened his mouth to ask if she was all right, but before he made a sound, she tripped backward, moonlight reflecting in the whites of her eyes as she toppled. Her head smacked against the trunk of the tree behind her with an unsettling thud.

"I'm not here to hurt you!" Alex called. The girl didn't move. *Oh, no.* He rushed forward and knelt beside her. Her eyes were closed, and she didn't stir, even when he tentatively reached out and touched her arm. No, not a girl. A young, fair-skinned woman. Short, perhaps Meredith's height, but definitely a young woman. An attractive one, despite the scarlet hue to his vision.

He gulped. "Um, can you hear me?"

The young woman didn't stir, so he gently shook her shoulder. Still nothing. But her chest rose and fell slightly, and he sensed her warmth. She was alive, at least. He never would have forgiven himself if he'd saved her, only to frighten her to death.

Alex sat back on his heels. Now what? He couldn't leave her. What was she doing all alone in the mountains? The scent of horse lingered in the area, but the animal must have bolted when the wolves attacked. He looked around and inhaled deeply. No sign or scent of any other humans, just a worn-down area of grass where horse and woman must have been pacing.

But she owned a horse. Or had stolen one. Judging by the fine make of her embroidered dress and cloak, it seemed more likely she was wealthy enough to own one. Maybe she had gotten lost or separated from a caravan. Unfortunately, he had no way of knowing where she might have been headed or where to find any companions she might or might not have.

Not that it mattered. Even if she had companions and he knew where they were, he couldn't exactly walk up to a group of humans in all his cursed dragon-man glory and hand them an unconscious, injured girl and expect to walk away unscathed.

The scent of blood grew stronger. He looked her over, ignoring the dragon's hunger as he searched for the source. A scratch on her arm had scabbed over, but her right boot was punctured and sticky with fresh blood. And she had hit her head pretty hard. She needed help. Meredith would know what to do.

So Alex did the only thing he could. He picked her up and flew back to the cave.

2

Alex knocked his boot against Meredith and Peter's door, the young woman still unconscious in his arms. She had curled against him, probably seeking his heat. How stupid was it that he liked how that felt? The pressure of her body against his; the protective instinct it stirred in his chest.

A few moments passed, so he kicked at the door again. Inside, Peter muttered something unintelligible, then flint scraped. After a moment, a bleary-eyed, wild-haired Peter answered the door, clutching a candle.

"I need help." Alex looked down at the girl in his arms. "She's hurt."

Peter stared at the young woman in stunned silence, his face pale in the candlelight. "Who…what…"

"I need Meredith," Alex said.

"What's going…" Meredith shuffled up next to her husband and froze, her mouth hanging open. "Who's this?"

"I don't know." Alex gazed at the young woman's face, now illuminated by the flickering candle. She had soft features, with pink lips that were slightly parted as she breathed deeply. It had almost certainly been too long since he'd seen a girl, because she seemed too pretty to be real. He tamped down the thought and looked to Meredith.

"I was flying and heard her screaming. Found her surrounded

by wolves. One bit her ankle before I got there, and she's bleeding. Then she hit her head and hasn't woken up."

"Come on." Meredith took the candle from Peter and hurried out, still in her white nightgown. "We'll put her in Lucas's bed."

Meredith led the way with her candle, followed by Peter, while Alex trailed after them with the injured young woman. As if it had realized it wasn't about to break Alex's twelve-year stretch of not eating people, the dragon had gone back to sleep. Now if only Alex could silence the part of himself that kept drawing his gaze to the attractive girl in his arms.

Meredith opened Lucas's door, and Alex was glad it hadn't been locked. He didn't mind carrying the mysterious girl, but his arms were growing fatigued. Lucas mumbled something and rolled over, pulling his blanket up so high only the tousled ends of his brown hair were visible, but Meredith shook him awake.

"Wake up, dear. Come on. We need your bed; get up. That's it."

Lucas stumbled out of bed, eyes half closed as Peter prodded him out of the room. "Waz gon' on?" he asked his father.

Meredith pulled back the blankets, and Alex smirked as he laid the young woman in Lucas's bed. His best friend never did like being woken up in the middle of the night.

Peter gave Lucas a gentle shove out the door. "Alex found a girl—"

"A girl?" Lucas suddenly sounded more awake.

"No, you're leaving her alone; she's hurt." Peter and Lucas's voices faded down the tunnels.

Meredith shooed Alex aside, her auburn braid slipping over her shoulder as she bent over the blonde. "Alex…" She traced her fingertips over the embroidery on the young woman's dress. "This is not a peasant girl."

Alex nodded, hoping Meredith wasn't upset with him for bringing a potentially dangerous stranger into their home. "Is she all right, though?"

Meredith looked up at him with a soft smile. "I'll take care of her. Go fetch some water and bandages and rags, please."

Alex hurried off to do as asked. When he returned, Meredith had removed the young woman's ripped cloak, as well as her gloves and boots, and had arranged her more comfortably on the bed.

"How hard did she hit her head?" Meredith asked as she took the supplies. "She barely awoke enough to say 'Gareth,' and then passed out again."

"It sounded hard." He swallowed and looked at the floor. "I frightened her."

Meredith sighed. "You said she was being attacked by wolves and alone in the mountains. She was already frightened." She set about cleaning the girl's ankle.

Alex sat on Lucas's stool and watched, his tail twitching. The blonde moaned and shifted but didn't wake up, and his worry grew. He hadn't meant to scare her. What if she'd hit her head too hard to wake up again?

"Nightmare?" Meredith asked softly, intruding on his thoughts.

He adjusted his wings and brushed at a crumb on the table. Meredith glanced at him knowingly. He couldn't deny it, so he grunted something vaguely affirmative.

"Do you want to talk about it?"

The scales on his tail rasped as it swished over the stone. He wasn't about to admit Henry had put a sword through his chest this time. That didn't usually happen. Or that Lucas was there. One of his family—friends, really, but they felt like family—sometimes appeared in the dreams, but the worst was when they agreed with Henry, like Lucas had in the most recent torment.

Meredith gave Alex that look of pity that made him feel like a child again, but she didn't push. His exhaustion finally caught up to him, so he rested his head on his forearm on the table. The young woman looked angelically peaceful in her sleep, and Alex hoped that meant she wouldn't have lasting damage from her fall. He didn't remember dozing off, but he awoke to Meredith rubbing his back between his wings.

She stepped back as he stretched out a crick in his neck. "Is she going to be all right?"

"She's moved and opened her eyes a couple times. I think she's just exhausted and overwhelmed but is going to be fine," Meredith said. "The bite on her ankle isn't terrible, and otherwise it's only scratches. A bit of a bump on the back of her head, but she's not feverish and is sleeping all right, so I'm optimistic."

"Good, good. She has nothing on her? No supplies?" He frowned at the slumbering form of the young woman, now covered by Lucas's blanket. *Who are you, and what happened to you?* "Perhaps she got separated from a group. I smelled horse but no other humans."

Meredith shook her head.

Alex stood. "Thank you for taking care of her."

"Of course. You did the right thing, bringing her back here." Meredith smiled at him. "Very heroic and charming."

He raised his brows. "She needed help…"

"Yes. Just…girls like being rescued." Meredith winked. "Maybe—"

Heat that had nothing to do with the dragon flashed over his cheeks. "Stop. Just…stop. The look in her eyes…she was terrified of me, Mer. And…just, no."

Meredith's expression saddened. "All right." But the glimmer of hope didn't fade from her eyes. He kissed her forehead and trudged back to his own room, Meredith's unspoken suggestion like a weight around his neck.

None of their hope changed what he knew to be true.

His curse couldn't be broken. He felt it, deep down. Even if it were otherwise…

No beautiful young woman would ever love a monster.

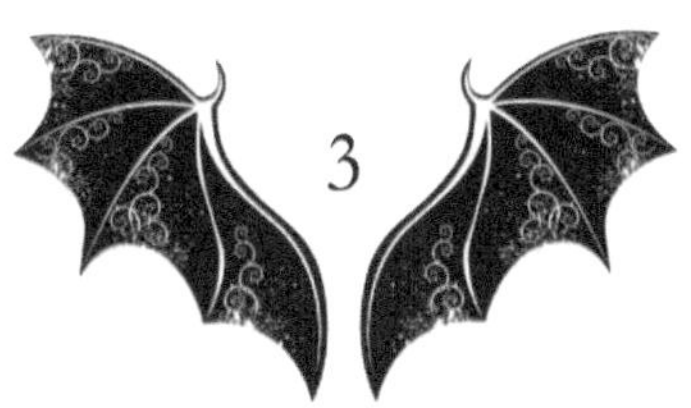

3

Alex's stomach woke him. After being up half the night, he could have lain in bed much longer, but he suspected he'd already slept in—even though he couldn't be sure deep inside the cave. He slipped on his boots and plodded to the dining room. To his surprise and relief, the others were just putting down place settings.

"Morn—" A yawn interrupted his words as Alex collapsed into his chair at the head of the table. "Morning," he repeated while absently adjusting his wings on either side of the narrow back of his chair. "Is the girl awake?"

Meredith smiled at him as she placed a steaming tray of omelets on the table. "Good morning. I checked on her before I started making breakfast, and she wasn't awake."

"I just peeked in on her before coming in," Jasper said as he passed around utensils. "Still sleeping peacefully."

"Everyone has seen her but me." Lucas crossed his arms and slouched down in his chair. He hadn't combed his mousy brown hair yet, and it was a mess.

"You'd wake her up," Alex said with a laugh. "Besides, you hardly look presentable."

"Well maybe she'd want breakfast. And who cares what I look like?" Lucas tossed his hands in the air. "Mom said she was hurt and all dirty, anyway."

To Alex's left, Jasper leaned forward in his chair and tapped his fingers on the tabletop. "True, but there's a strong chance she's a noble, so if you *are* given the opportunity to meet her, you might want to at least comb your hair."

"A *noble?*" Lucas sat up straighter. "Why do you think that? Did she say something? How exactly did you find her again, Alex? Did she talk to you before she passed out? Where—"

"All right, slow down." Alex rubbed his forehead, but despite how tired he was, and how overwhelming Lucas's penchant for incessant questions was, he couldn't help but smile. "She's dressed really well, is all. And…" He shook his head. "Too many questions. What were the rest?"

"Eat some food." Meredith transferred an omelet from the tray to a plate and set it in front of him before settling into her own chair. Alex tried not to let it bother him. She only served him his food when she was worried about him.

"And then you can tell us the whole story," Peter said as he helped himself to breakfast.

Jasper nodded as he also served himself. "I'd like all the details as well. Meredith and Peter told me what they knew, but I have many questions."

Alex took several bites before starting his story, but he didn't dare wait until he was finished, as Lucas looked ready to bounce off his chair with impatience.

"I had a nightmare," Alex said quietly. Meredith had probably already told Peter and Jasper, and they'd likely put it together, anyway, so there was no point in hiding it. "I needed some air and went flying."

"You could have woken me up." Lucas stilled, looking at Alex with concern. "I keep telling you I don't mind."

Alex smiled weakly at his adoptive brother. He had woken Lucas last time, and even though Lucas had fallen asleep on him, the company had helped. But it wouldn't have helped with this last nightmare.

"I know," Alex said. "I needed to get out of the cave more than I needed to talk."

"We can talk outside."

A bit of irritation with Lucas's stubbornness sparked, but Alex smothered it. He considered admitting Lucas had been in his dream, but that would just make Lucas feel down even though it wasn't his fault, and Alex refused to put that burden on him. "I'll remember next time."

Lucas looked unconvinced, but he nodded and returned to eating.

"Anyway, I was flying, and I heard screaming and growling and smelled blood. I headed toward it—"

"A bit reckless, wasn't that?" Peter asked, eyes narrowed.

Alex forced himself to remain tall and regal and keep his voice even. "I'm not a child anymore. And I'm half dragon. Besides, it was one woman, and she was clearly in distress."

Peter considered him for a moment, then nodded. Jasper's mouth twisted, as if he were trying to decide if he wanted to frown or smile.

"I roared and scared off the wolves that had her surrounded, but before I got a chance to say anything, she saw me, and…" Alex prodded his omelet with his fork. "She backed away, tripped, and hit her head. There wasn't anyone else around, not even the scent of other humans, just of a horse that was no longer there, and she was unconscious and bleeding. I flew back here. That's the story."

Lucas's shoulders slumped. He'd probably been hoping for a more theatrical tale.

After breakfast, Lucas desperately wanted to see the mysterious girl, but Peter talked him into a sword-fighting lesson instead.

Meredith had planned on spending the day baking, so Jasper went to check on the young woman. After a few moments' hesitation, Alex followed him.

Alex peeked through the open door. Jasper leaned over the bed, the back of his fingers held to the young woman's forehead. After adjusting her blanket, Jasper stepped back. The young woman stirred but didn't wake, so Alex stepped inside, drawing closer to the crackling fire.

"She's still sleeping?"

"Yes, but lightly." Jasper turned toward Alex. "Do you want to meet her when she wakes?"

Alex rustled his wings and his tail twitched. The idea of meeting someone new was tantalizing, but… "Would that be wise?"

"You *did* save her life." Jasper shrugged his bowed shoulders. "And…well, she's a woman. You know the legends. There's always a chance—"

"No." The word held more bite than Alex had intended. Would he have to have this argument with everyone? "But I *am* curious… I haven't talked to anyone new in so long…" Jasper watched him steadily, hopeful but not pressuring, and Alex caved. "I'll meet her, but only to talk and to help her get home," he said with a bit of warning.

Jasper nodded, although disappointment flickered in his eyes. "I suppose we'll have to be careful what we say, then. A girl in those clothes, with such soft hands and silky hair…she's wealthy, almost certainly noble. You know how nobility like to gossip."

He met Alex's eyes, and he didn't need to speak aloud his fears. If the woman told the Rethali court she'd met Prince Alexander Tallon in the mountains, revealing that Henry had lied about killing him twelve years ago, Henry would have no choice but to hunt him down. The mountains would be crawling with hunting parties looking to slay the monster prince.

Alex clenched his teeth as he shoved down his fears and anger and focused on the lovely young woman. "But why would a noblewoman be alone in the mountains? What if she's in some kind of trouble?"

"Perhaps she could reside here for a time." Jasper said it casually, although Alex wondered if the old steward was secretly hoping for that outcome.

"I won't tell her who I am, to be safe. I just want to help her get home. Assuming she has a home to go to, which I hope she does." No one deserved to be driven from their home.

"A selfless choice, my prince." Jasper had that annoying expression of pride again—a look Alex both loved and hated. Loved because it always bolstered him; hated, because he never would be the king Jasper was set on him becoming.

Alex gave a half smile in return and left the room and the mysterious girl behind to go check the fishing traps.

Now that he'd thought about meeting her, he desperately wanted to, partly out of curiosity and partly out of a morbid fascination with how she would react. Other than his adoptive family, only a couple hunters had seen him in twelve years. Unless he counted a few peasant children who had spotted him in dragon form, which he didn't. The hunters had not taken seeing him well. But safe in a cave, away from imminent danger, after he had saved her…maybe it would be different. He longed to talk to someone new. The others got to visit the village. Alex just got to be lonely while they were gone.

By dinner, Alex was back to worrying that the young woman would never wake. Lucas was a little concerned, too, since she had taken over his bed. But mid-afternoon, Jasper knocked on Alex's door and walked in without waiting.

"She's awake."

Alex tossed the book he hadn't really been reading onto his bed and leapt to his feet. His wings unfurled in his haste, but he folded them back down. As he followed Jasper back to Lucas's room, his nerves wound tight, which made the dragon stir in his chest. He ignored it.

For the first time in twelve years, he was going to talk to a new person.

4

While they walked to Lucas's room, Jasper filled him in on what the girl had said to him. She did have a family, who she claimed were on the pass. That brought Alex some comfort, until he added that the girl had mentioned there'd been some kind of attack. Perhaps that explained how Alex had found her so far from the pass. Hopefully her family was all right.

Jasper opened the door and walked into Lucas's room, stepping out of Alex's way so he could enter as well. The young woman rose from the stool at the table as her gaze moved from Jasper to Alex. Her dazzling blue eyes widened as she pressed her hand over her mouth and backed away until she tripped backward onto the bed.

Alex tried to hide his disappointment while he stepped further into the room, but his wings gave an anxious jerk, anyway.

"Stay back!" The woman pressed against the wall, holding out a hand as if to ward him off.

Alex's face heated. He'd known she might see a monster, but it was more difficult than anticipated. Henry's face flashed through his mind, taunting him. *Abomination.* He pushed the memory of his uncle away.

"I'm not going to hurt you," he reassured her. "You can stop cowering."

"What are you?" The young woman's voice shook as she continued to press against the wall like it offered some measure of protection.

19

He shouldn't have come, but it was too late now. Maybe if he acted like a normal person, she would realize he wasn't a monster. "I'm Alexander." He tried to smile, but it felt forced. "And you are...?"

She didn't answer, just stared at him, registering all his monstrous features—his horns, claws, wings, and tail. She shuddered and stared at her skirt. He sighed.

"I guess I don't really need your name since you won't be here long."

The girl swallowed. "Please d-don't eat me."

"Eat..." His agitation grew, and his tail thrashed. He still had a human face and body. Did he really look like the kind of creature that ate girls? "I—"

"I can get you gold!" The young woman wrapped her arms around her knees and looked up at him, but her whole frame shook. "Jewels or—"

"Oh, hush." He should have stayed away, and not just because of her fear. Fire grew in his stomach. *Stay calm.*

"I'm not lying!" Firelight glistened in her unshed tears, and guilt twisted Alex's heart. "If you let me go—"

"I *am* letting you go." Alex stepped aside and motioned past Jasper at the open doorway, his anger flaring. Anger at her, at himself, at Jasper for talking him into this debacle. Rage at his uncle for making him into something that terrified pretty girls. "I *was* going to ask you where you were headed and offer to take you there, but never mind. Just go."

"Alex," Jasper interrupted in his patient advisor tone, with just a hint of warning.

Alex huffed and lowered his arm. Right. He should still be polite. "Jasper says you were traveling with your family? How were you separated?"

The blonde looked up at him with resolve, even though her voice still squeaked a little as she spoke. "We were attacked by a manticore in Thetlane Pass. My horse spooked and ran away."

For a moment, confusion clouded Alex's thoughts. "Thet—" Of course. It had been a while since he'd heard the name. "Oh, you mean Gonah Way. You're from Eynlae." How interesting, although a little embarrassing that the possibility hadn't occurred to him.

"Yes." She peered at the open door and didn't seem inclined to share more.

"Were you headed into or out of Rethalyon?" Alex prodded.

"To Rethalyon." A disappointing answer, as Eynlae would have been safer. The young woman took several deep breaths. Alex waited, trying not to pressure her. "I want to leave now."

Of course she did. He nodded. "If you're up to traveling."

"I…" She rubbed her arm and glanced at Jasper. *She must trust him, since he isn't…me.* "I don't know the way," she admitted.

Alex grunted and mussed his hair, his fingers bumping against the base of his horns. He should have guessed a lost noblewoman would need a guide. Besides, he'd said he wanted to help her, and the truth was, even though her fear grated on him, he did want to help.

"Where were you headed?" he asked, hoping it wasn't far.

The young woman seemed to consider for a moment, calculations flying behind those bright blue eyes. "Hathlon," she said at last, "but my family is on the pass."

Every muscle in Alex's body tensed as memories tried to resurface. "The royal town. Why?"

"Does it matter?" She straightened, and nobility radiated from her.

Concern spread in Alex's chest, and the dragon twitched in response to his rising emotions.

"If my family survived," she continued, "they will be looking for me near the pass. If you take me to them, you'll be rewarded. Gold…gems…whatever you want."

Alex growled, failing to ignore the offense. "And I'd want gold because I'm a dragon?" Heat snaked into his chest, mocking him. *Yes, you are a dragon.*

"N-no. Because you're…a man. Men…like riches."

An impressive save, but he could tell she didn't mean it.

"What do you desire?" She sucked in a breath. "We weren't travelling with much gold, but we can get more. I swear it. Whatever you want, you'll have it."

His eyes narrowed. Who was this girl? This wasn't just any noble if she thought she could get him those things so easily.

"Please. Once we arrive at the palace—"

Alex couldn't stop his snarl or the acrid smoke that puffed from his nostrils. If this girl told Henry where he was… "Palace? Who are you?"

She closed her eyes without answering.

"Tell me!" The words erupted in a roar of smoke. The dragon was restless in his chest, eager to take control and face whatever danger Alex feared.

"Alex." Even Jasper's voice did little to quell his rising panic and the urge to shift.

The girl opened her eyes.

"Who are you?" Alex demanded. "What's your business at the palace?" He bared his teeth, struggling to keep the dragon at bay as all his darkest fears and deepest hurts threatened to overwhelm him.

"Raelyn Argent!" She lifted her chin, defiant even as she trembled. "I am the Princess of Eynlae on my way to marry Crown Prince Tristan Carbrey."

Alex staggered back. She might as well have kicked him. *Princess of Eynlae…Tristan…* That—that couldn't be possible.

"Deliver me to my family safely," the princess insisted, "and you will be rewarded."

Jasper cleared his throat. "A word outside, Alexan—"

"Quiet!" Alex wasn't in the mood for Jasper's unwavering calm or methodical logic. His wings jerked as he struggled to snuff out the dragon ire burning in his stomach.

"You'll marry the princess of Eynlae," his father's voice, at least as well as he remembered it, echoed in his mind. Henry couldn't stop at taking his parents, his life, his crown, and his home. He had to take his wife, too. White-hot flames roiled in his gut.

"Princess Raelyn of Eynlae," Alex repeated. "Betrothed to the *crown prince.*" He couldn't control his growl, and he didn't really want to. *Betrothed to me. Now to my usurping uncle's son.* "Are you telling me the truth?" Part of him desperately hoped it was a lie. Scales pricked through his skin on the back of his neck as he stepped closer. The girl crawled to the far corner of the bed. "Are you the princess?"

She hung her head. "No—"

"Then why did you say you were?" Smoke pushed out of his mouth. Was she a liar? Trying to manipulate him?

"I lied!" Her admission both relieved and angered him further. "I'm sorry. I thought I could trick you—"

Too much trickery. He seized her arm, determined to have the truth.

"No, wait, please!" She struggled for a moment, then stilled as he tightened his grip.

Jasper moved into his periphery. "Alexander, stop!"

I have to know. He was too incensed to feel much guilt as he yanked the girl to her feet and placed his hand against the side of her neck. "Tell me the truth. What's your name?"

"Raelyn! Princess Raelyn Argent." A furious sort of calm settled over the princess as she met his eyes. "And if you hurt me, my brother will *kill you.*"

He sensed her honesty as if he had glimpsed into her heart. The woman he was to marry, engaged to his cousin, terrified of Alex and confident in her brother's ability to kill a monster. His betrothed…now the future daughter-in-law of his parents' killer. More scales sliced through his skin under his shirt. "Princess indeed."

Alex pushed her away and stalked toward the door. Now what?

If he let her go, she would tell Henry. He'd be in danger, and so would his family. *I told them I shouldn't meet her!* If Princess Raelyn married Tristan, though, she might be in danger, too. Who knew what Henry might do to a defenseless princess if it got him what he wanted? Alex's tail pounded against the stone as the dragon's anger burned hotter at the idea of Henry causing anyone more pain.

"I've changed my mind. She stays." His voice rumbled. The dragon was ready to emerge.

Jasper looked more disappointed than surprised. "Don't be rash."

"She'd tell him!" He motioned back in Raelyn's general direction but didn't have the time for any more explanation. "She. Stays."

"People are looking for me," the princess argued.

"Lock her in." Alex hurried out of the room as his muscles twitched with the painful sharpness that always preceded a shift. *Get the clothes off, get out—*

"Alexander!" Jasper's voice stopped him. "Get back here!"

Alex ground his teeth, but that was *not* a suggestion. Ignoring Jasper always earned him a lecture on accepting advice and not being impetuous, and he didn't want to add a berating to everything else. So he stomped back inside and crossed his arms, scowling at his tutor. "What?" He felt scales push through his cheeks. There was no stopping the shift now.

"You're losing control," Jasper said, as if Alex wasn't painfully aware of that. "And you manhandled a lady."

A bit of shame pricked him, and he glanced toward the sobbing princess. His remorse increased, but it wasn't enough to stop the change spreading through him, drowning out most of his emotions with dragon fury. "Hence why I'm *leaving*." *Before I do anything worse.*

"Not until you apologize to Princess Raelyn."

The surge of annoyance was like a match to dry tinder. Alex threw his head back and released the flames. He didn't have time for this.

"Stop being a child," Jasper said in that tone that conveyed he thought Alex was better than this.

He's wrong. Now that the dragon was surfacing, it wanted destruction. A mocking voice in his head insisted he stop pretending that it wasn't him, that the dragon was something separate from his own pain and anger, and that just made him feel worse. "I need to go."

"Better apologize quickly, then."

Alex snorted, smoke billowing out of his nose. He glared at the princess, and his body ached and strained as he fought the shift. "I apologize for grabbing you and treating you roughly, Princess." A searing pain cut through his torso. He groaned and ran away before it was too late.

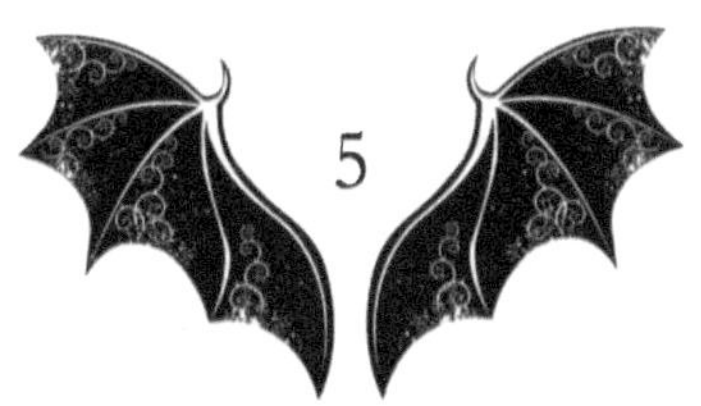

5

Alex didn't make it far before he collapsed on all fours, kicking off his boots. His hands shook as he struggled to pull his trousers off, but he was out of time. Agony tore through his muscles as his body grew and twisted. His clothes shredded. Meredith wouldn't be pleased. He let his dragon form take over, his rage sharpening.

Make her pay, the dragon part of his mind growled. *The princess who dares treat you like a monster, who reminded you of everything you lost.*

He roared to silence the voice. It wasn't the princess's fault. He flew out of the cave, focusing on the wind beneath his wings and the scents of the trees and lakes and creatures roaming the forests.

The princess of Eynlae.

What were the chances he would find *her,* of all people?

And why did she have to be so beautiful? In another life, they would be getting married in a few days, and he would be thanking the stars for his luck. In this one, she would never look at him without fear, hatred, or both.

Alex released another roar to combat his burning rage.

It wasn't all anger, he knew. It was heartbreak and guilt and loss and dread. But the dragon best understood wrath.

He spied a lake and dove toward it, even though the dragon screamed *no.* The frigid water shocked his system and turned his energy toward keeping him warm. He crawled out of the lake, still in dragon form but more in control, and curled up on the shore.

Over a year had passed since his last incident. Usually he controlled it—he'd think about what he was feeling and why, or latch onto one of his friends and focus on them until he could calm himself and subdue the dragon. But the tumult of emotions from talking to Princess Raelyn…

He hadn't been able to control it fast enough.

Maybe a part of him hadn't wanted to.

Alex sighed and rested his chin on a massive forepaw. What was he going to do now? He couldn't risk going anywhere near the palace or being seen by anyone else in Raelyn's family—assuming they were alive. Alex chided himself for the relief that the idea of Raelyn's family being gone had brought, and also promptly dismissed the possibility. A royal family on their way to a royal wedding would have a large retinue of skilled knights, and while manticores were nasty beasts, they were not of the variety that had impenetrable hides. A relatively easy kill, and the royals would have stayed well away from the fighting.

Even if he were careful in returning her to her family, by the way she had looked at him…she would tell. Perhaps not right away, but sooner or later, the princess would let something slip about the dragon-man in the mountains. When she did, Henry would put it together.

Perhaps Henry would want to kill Alex before the lords found out that he lied, or perhaps the lords would learn of it and demand Alex be hunted down. Alex hadn't attacked anyone in twelve years of being cursed, but it wouldn't matter. According to Henry, the court couldn't suffer a monster to live. Either way, Alex would be hunted, and his family would be in danger. He wasn't about to let some girl ruin the life they had literally carved out of the mountain.

Not to mention the entire situation didn't make sense. According to Jasper, Henry had argued with Alex's father on more than one occasion *against* the treaty with the Eynlaeans. It was one of many things that Henry had criticized King Philip for. They'd learned years ago that Henry had renegotiated the treaty—Jasper had wondered about it for weeks—but somehow, it had never occurred to Alex that the new treaty would have changed Raelyn's future betrothed to…*Tristan.* A bit of a growl rumbled through his scale-covered body.

What was that feeling…jealousy? Surely not. It was an arranged marriage one way or the other, and he'd never met Raelyn before. Tristan likely hadn't, either. No, it wasn't jealousy; it was…*injustice.* His clearest memory of Tristan was of his cousin's callousness at Alex's mother's funeral. Even a lying princess who thought Alex looked like he ate girls for supper didn't deserve Tristan as a husband and Henry as a father-in-law.

Somehow, Alex had to make Princess Raelyn understand why she couldn't leave. Yes, convince a princess that a monster was telling her the truth about how villainous a king was, and that she was safer and better off in a cave than in a castle.

This was going to be a disaster.

Alex rested on the shoreline. He didn't let himself fall asleep, his ears and nose on alert for any approaching humans, but he enjoyed letting the sunlight warm his scales. Even as the sun dipped low, he didn't get up. Once he returned home, he'd need to talk to Princess Raelyn. Worse, Jasper would be disappointed in him. Alex hated disappointing Jasper. And he did it a lot lately, as he'd struggled to show interest in keeping up with pointless kingship studies.

At last the growing chill in the dusk air and his empty belly drove him home. The flight was quick as a dragon. After he shifted back into his human form, he tried to sneak into his bedroom without seeing anyone. To his chagrin, however, Jasper was sitting in the dining room in front of the crackling fire, facing the entryway with his hands folded on his lap, waiting.

6

"I want to be dressed for this conversation," Alex muttered as he strode through the dining room without pausing.

"Understandable," Jasper said amicably.

Alex barely restrained himself from rolling his eyes. He took his time getting dressed, delaying the inevitable, but he couldn't even dress himself entirely on his own. Blasted wings and claws. He sulked back out to the dining hall.

"Would you please help me?" Embarrassment made his voice sound pathetic.

Jasper eased out of his chair with a poorly hidden, pained groan. If there was one thing Alex wanted more than he wanted his curse to break, he wished he could make Jasper feel better. He wished that instead of being able to tell if someone was lying when he touched them, he could take Jasper's pain. Instead of healing any of his own wounds when he shifted, he wished he could heal Jasper's hunched back and achy joints—or bring back Leanna, Jasper's deceased wife. But he couldn't.

He couldn't even live up to the expectations Jasper had of him.

"I'm sorry," Alex whispered as Jasper did up the buttons on the back of Alex's shirt beneath his wings.

"I'm not the one you need to apologize to."

Alex tapped his claws against his leg. "I did let you down, though."

"So you did." Jasper said it matter-of-factly, without judgment or condemnation. "But now you must decide what you do next. Besides, I know you tried. And I know that must have hurt a lot. Both literally and emotionally."

Alex nodded, his throat tight.

"Are you hungry?" Jasper asked as he finished off the buttons.

Alex turned to face him. "Starved."

"Good." Jasper smiled. "The princess hasn't eaten yet, either. Perhaps you would like to invite her to supper?"

If the princess wasn't likely to yell at him or cower again, Alex would have gladly invited the beautiful young woman to supper. As it was, that sounded like an excellent way to ruin his meal. But Jasper stood there looking at him expectantly, and as much as he wanted to deny it, Alex couldn't very well keep Princess Raelyn in the cave and not speak to her.

"This isn't a suggestion, is it?"

Jasper's smile deepened, crinkling his eyes. "Consider it a strongly advised suggestion. If you want to keep her here, then you need to be hospitable. And difficult conversations are often easier over food. We have meals set aside for both of you, so all you have to do is go politely ask her to join you. Show her who you really are. It will also give you an opportunity for a proper apology."

Alex grunted. Difficult to argue with that. "Very well."

Jasper retrieved a torch from next to the fireplace, and they walked to Lucas's room. Jasper knocked, but the princess didn't answer or make a sound. He knocked again. Still nothing. The judgmental royal was probably ignoring them.

"Just open it," Alex grumbled.

Jasper's lips pursed. "Do you want her to feel like a guest or a prisoner?"

"She *is* my prisoner, technically." Alex regretted the words even before Jasper gave him an exasperated look.

"Alex."

Jasper's "I believe you're better than this" stares were entirely unfair, and in that moment, made Alex rather peevish. Alex stepped up to the door and banged the side of his hand against it. If that didn't get the princess's attention, he was going to go back to the dining room and eat on his own. Behind him, Jasper sighed.

Princess Raelyn's muffled voice sounded from inside the room. "What do you want?"

Some royal manners his former betrothed had. Alex frowned. "I'm not shouting at you through this door."

After a moment of listening, he heard movement inside. Then the princess opened the door, squinting against the torchlight.

Be polite, Alex; you can do this.

"Princess." Alex briefly bowed his head. "Would you join me for supper?"

Her guarded stance didn't relax. If anything, she looked more on edge. "I'm tired. You woke me."

"Oh." He probably should have realized that's why she wasn't answering. *Idiot.* "I apologize. Well, you're awake now. Do you want to eat?"

Wariness flashed over her features as she drew back. "I'd rather eat alone."

He'd expected her fear, and yet, it still cut him deeply. "I'm not going to eat *you*, if that's what you're worried about."

"Why would you dine with your *prisoner*?" She crossed her arms, that regal air creeping into her bearing again.

And...she'd overheard him. Superb. Still, she didn't have to be so condescending. "Fine. Don't eat then."

Jasper cleared his throat.

Alex managed to stop his groan by staring up at the ceiling and breathing for a moment. He needed to be a friendly human to have any hope of winning her over. He looked back at Princess Raelyn's distractingly pretty face. "Please. I want you to be my guest. Dine with me?"

"I want to dine with my family."

She couldn't know how those quiet words gutted him. He'd lost one family and lived every day with the fear that he would lose his current one, and he hated himself for keeping this innocent girl from hers. But what choice did he have? He couldn't think of a way to reunite the princess with her loved ones—and Henry and Tristan—without endangering his own.

Something like resignation settled into Princess Raelyn's expression, and she started to close the door.

Desperate, Alex put out his hand and stopped the door, trying to ignore the way she flinched as he did so. He just needed her to understand. "Dine with me," he murmured, "and I'll explain. I'll try to answer the questions you must have."

An internal war played out in her eyes, but then her stomach growled, and that seemed to push her over. "All right."

Alex saved his smile for after he had turned and was leading the way to the dining room. She was talking to him, at least, and with minimal cowering. And she was hungry. Who wasn't more irritable and on edge when they were hungry? Maybe with some food in her—and seeing that Alex ate food like a normal person—she would warm up to him enough to listen. And then, surely, she would have to understand.

Unfortunately, things got off to a rough start. The princess refused to sit next to him, even moving a chair to sit on the opposite end of the table. The slight stoked the dragon's rage, so he focused on eating and calming the unwarranted irritation. Jasper stood off to the side in the shadows, providing a much-needed anchor and silent support.

Alex had barely quelled the fire in his chest when the princess asked, "How long have I been here?"

"A day."

Even across the table, he saw how her grip tightened on her fork. "Why didn't you just take me to the pass?"

Alex tilted his head. The princess didn't seem unintelligent. Surely she could puzzle out why he would avoid the pass. But, partly thanks to Jasper's lurking presence, Alex curbed his snark and spoke patiently. "Why would I have done that? I never go near the pass. I found you far from there, alone, unconscious, and bleeding. So I took you where I knew I could get help."

"Help?" Incredulity rang in the single word, and he could see her trying to reconcile his appearance with an act of kindness.

Alex spoke before he thought better of it. "How shocking that a *monster* would give you aid." He stabbed his venison harder than necessary, aggravated with himself and already anticipating Jasper's reproach.

"Tone, Alexander." There it was. Jasper's quiet voice might as well have been a shout for how chided Alex felt. "And the thing we discussed…"

Alex slouched. "I'm sorry for grabbing you. And for frightening you." Oh, dragon fire, he hadn't hurt her, had he? "Is your arm all right?"

Princess Raelyn looked across the table at him, feeling her arm. "Yes."

"Good. Good." As long as they were having awkward conversations, maybe he should explain his reaction. He tapped his claws against his goblet, gathering his courage. How should he approach this? He said the first thing that popped into his mind. "You're engaged to the crown prince."

Caution radiated from the princess. "Yes."

"Do you want to marry him?" It was an irrelevant question to what he needed to tell her, but he found himself deeply curious. Besides, if she were dreading the marriage, maybe his news would be welcome.

Her lips parted, as if the question surprised her. Then her fear came back as she looked away. Alex thought he should be getting used to her fright, but every time, it hurt.

"Of course," she said.

So much for the hope she wanted out of the marriage. "Why? Have you met him?"

The princess took a drink. Stalling, probably, based on how her hand was shaking. "No, I haven't. But I've heard he is brave, capable, and handsome."

Right. Unlike Alex. If she chose to be shallow, he could, too. "Let's not forget *handsome*." Oh, he was royally messing this up. But something about the princess sitting there, beautiful even coated in dirt and blood and with her braid coming undone, combined with her obvious dislike and fear, seemed to have completely scrambled his mind.

"Marrying him will help keep the peace between Eynlae and Rethalyon." Confidence and a bit of challenge lent steel to Raelyn's retort. "That's the only thing I care about."

Alex didn't need to test her honesty to know the truth—the passion in her voice convinced him. She cared about her kingdom, and she had some fire in her. It was attractive. Alex quickly pushed that feeling aside. Clearly, Raelyn wasn't going to fall for him. The thought made him moody, because if she weren't so hostile, Alex could definitely see himself falling for her, with her sapphire eyes and quick thinking and sheer stubbornness—

"Please understand," the princess said, interrupting his thoughts.

"This marriage is required by a treaty that allows my people to use the trade routes through Rethalyon to the sea."

Oh, Alex understood. He'd learned about the treaty in his tedious lessons as a child, and Jasper had explained more during his tutoring. As Raelyn talked about the provisions of the treaty, Alex wondered if Henry had increased the levy, since he'd argued the treaty gave Rethalyon a bad deal. If he had, and Eynlae had agreed, that meant Eynlae was desperate, which Henry would doubtless see as weakness to be exploited. This poor girl had no idea the danger she'd been heading into.

"My entire life has prepared me to be queen of Rethalyon, to keep peace and ensure my people are not isolated." The princess turned a pleading expression on him. "Please, you have to let me go."

Alex knew how that felt—to have everything in your life leading toward one purpose, and then have that ripped away. But as much as he wished he could do the one thing that would wipe that anguish from her face, he couldn't. He returned his goblet to the table. "I can't do that."

"My family…they'll be worried. They might think I'm dead. That's not fair, and it leaves my father trying to salvage a treaty he can no longer fulfill."

Maybe he could put her mind at ease on at least one point. "The Carbreys can't break a treaty over a dead princess."

That fire returned to her eyes. "What is the point of keeping me here? Just help me find my family like Jasper said you would!"

"That was before." He just needed to stay calm and explain. How difficult could it be? All he needed to do was not lose his temper around a beautiful girl who hated the sight of him and who had at one time been betrothed to him but was now promised to his usurping uncle's son.

All right, so it would be difficult, but difficult wasn't *impossible.*

"Before you learned who I am?" Raelyn questioned. "Why does it matter to you? Please." The word was more accusatory than begging. "I *have* to marry the crown prince."

Alex snorted, and an embarrassing curl of smoke accompanied it. *I should be the crown prince. Not cold-hearted Tristan.* He forced himself to ignore her and eat, trying to smother the anger flickering in his chest.

The princess heaved a sigh. "Why are you keeping me here? At least tell me that."

Alex glanced toward Jasper. Maybe he should ask Jasper to explain, as the princess seemed to like him more. But Jasper raised a brow, clearly thinking Alex needed to be the one to tell her. Alex poked at his food, wishing Jasper wasn't right. "I suspect you won't like what I have to say."

"I don't like being held captive, so I'd expect not." There was that fight again. Was it wrong that Princess Raelyn's stubborn resolve made him both angry and more attracted to her? Probably.

The mix of confusing emotions was making the dragon restless. Alex leaned back and tried to keep his voice calm despite the dragon heat clawing at him. "I can't allow you to marry Tristan Carbrey."

Even with his attempt at a peaceful demeanor, her eyes widened. "What? Why not?"

"Because." Maintaining a stoic expression while smothering the dragon was getting harder, and he decided to blame his distraction for the stupid words that spilled out of his mouth. "You're my bride, not his."

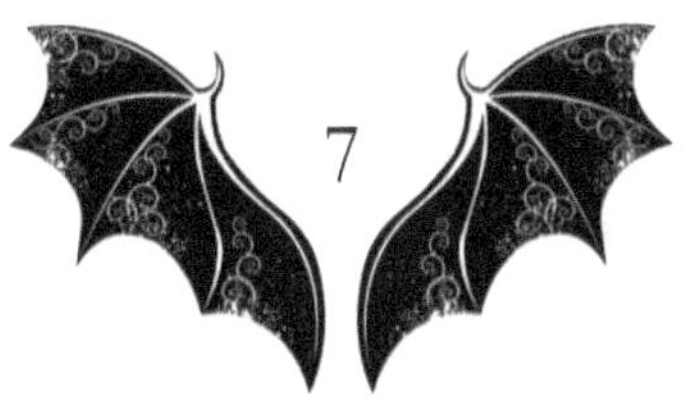

7

As it turned out, "you're my bride" was the worst way Alex could possibly have phrased telling Princess Raelyn the truth. She eventually calmed down and agreed to stay—after Alex chased her down before she ran into the heart of the mountain. He'd told her she would run into things that would actually eat her, and that wasn't strictly untrue…although the likelihood of her getting through the nets and spikes Alex and Peter had installed years ago to block off the tunnels that smelled strongly of monster was pretty small. All the same, running through tunnels that became more labyrinthine as they went deeper underground was a good plan if one wanted to get lost or injured. He'd felt so guilty for his brusqueness and so worried that she'd hurt herself that he'd barely even needed Jasper's prodding to go after her.

Of course, her continued distrust doused any friendly sentiments. It was like one of his nightmares come to life. Instead of the frightened, hateful looks and stabbing accusations of *monster* and people calling for his death being relegated to his memories and dreams, a petite princess had stood in his home, his haven, and called him a monster while brandishing a steak knife like she was contemplating putting it through his heart.

But then… She'd said his name. It had sounded wonderful, even though it was tainted by her shudder as she'd looked away from him.

By the time Alex went to bed, he was emotionally exhausted.

The girl was pretty and stubborn and educated and someone *new*, and all of that was exciting. But the princess of Eynlae was also frightened of him, and she felt like a living symbol of everything Henry's curse had taken. And when the dragon grew hot and protective in response to Alex's distress, that, too, was just another reminder of his loss.

The worst part was, even though he'd decided he wasn't a monster, even though his new family had spent the last twelve years telling him he was still human, and even though Jasper assured him that the fact that Alex tried so hard to fight the dragon's violent desires meant far more than the existence of the intrusive thoughts… When that heat grew in his chest, making him want to lash out, to make someone else suffer for his pain, it made Alex fear that he really was a monster.

The princess was at the table the next morning when Alex arrived for breakfast. He didn't acknowledge her at first, trying not to let the panicked look she sent his way as he entered the room ruin his morning. Instead, he greeted Lucas and Meredith and Peter and Jasper, exchanging laughter and smiles like they always did, but he could feel the princess's stare and the tension in the air. *I should probably try to be polite.*

However, his attempts at small talk—asking her how she slept and how her scraped hand and bitten ankle were faring—were met with brusque answers as she avoided looking at him. She could explain the difference between a diadem and a tiara to Lucas, but she could barely string two words together to Alex, forget meeting his eyes like a normal human being.

"Still can't look at me, hm?"

In response, all the princess did was glance across the table at him and look away with a poorly hidden shudder. She hated him—hated his very existence, as much as Henry ever had. Since they'd scarcely met, Alex knew Princess Raelyn's dislike shouldn't cut him as deeply as it did. All the same, her disgust hollowed him out, and anger gladly filled the emptiness.

"She'll get used to you," Meredith reassured him.

Alex cursed the weak flutter of hope that stirred at the idea.

Lucas was prattling on, and Peter hushed him. But Alex was focused on Princess Raelyn, who was ignoring her food. *Make conversation. Say something.*

"Do you have different fare in Eynlae?" he inquired. "Or am I so off-putting?" He immediately wished he could snatch the bitter words back.

"Leave the girl alone, Alex," Jasper said, ever the one to take the high road. Well, easy for Jasper to say. The princess wasn't side-eying Jasper with terror-fueled hostility.

"She could at least *try* to act like she doesn't hate the sight of me." A traitorous growl rumbled in Alex's chest. "She's making me angry."

Meredith flicked a chiding look toward him. "No, you're making yourself angry."

Alex was too grumpy to admit she was right. Blaming the princess seemed easier right then. "She's not helping," he protested. Or…maybe his resentment was making him imagine things that weren't there, and everyone thought he was over-reacting. If he weren't imagining things, perhaps if they heard it from her own lips, they wouldn't judge his sour mood. "Do I repulse you, Princess?"

Finally, the princess looked at Alex. His breath caught as she studied him. Did she know how pretty she was?

"No."

The single word from the princess stunned him, his jaw hanging so low it threatened to come unhinged. He *had* misjudged her. "I…" But the princess sat stiffly in her chair, the flames from the fireplace reflecting in her wide eyes.

"You're a good liar," he muttered.

She shook her head. "I'm too afraid to lie to you. You scare me, but you're not repulsive."

How he longed for that to be true, but he had the distinct feeling she was lying to his face. Perhaps to try to win his goodwill? If she both thought he was repulsive and that he wouldn't realize she was lying, that was a double insult. He stood and stalked toward her, ignoring Jasper and Meredith's attempts to stop him. The princess's manipulative games needed to end.

"I want the truth." Alex ignored the aching part of his heart that wanted the truth to be that she didn't find him repulsive. *Scary* he thought he could overcome. *Repulsive* would be harder.

"I told you the truth."

He would know for certain soon enough. Princess Raelyn shrank away from him, but sitting down, she couldn't avoid him as he placed his hand on the side of her neck. "Do you find me repulsive?" he repeated. It was petty, but at that moment, he didn't care what the princess or his family thought of his childish behavior— he just wanted, no *needed*, to know.

"No."

Deception. The dragon thrashed in Alex's mind, outraged at the mockery of its intelligence. "Liar." He drew away his hand with a snarl. This anger was dangerous, he knew that, but sometimes… Sometimes anger was so much easier to feel than hurt.

The princess paled, her eyes pleading as she trembled, looking up at him like he might roast her alive. The terror on her face softened his heart.

"You're terrifying her, Alexander." Meredith patted his shoulder, and the touch helped drive away the heat.

Cold shame coiled in Alex's stomach. Protecting himself with anger wasn't worth it when his anger scared and hurt others. He hadn't just been petty in forcing Raelyn to reveal the truth; he'd been cruel and intimidating and everything he didn't want to be. He crumpled. "Forgive me, Princess."

The words sounded hollow, and the princess must have thought the same, because she simply stared at him.

"Please?" he practically begged. *Give me another chance.*

But instead of answering, Princess Raelyn fixated on her skirt.

His spirits sank further into dejection. "Is that a no to forgiving me?"

The princess didn't look up or answer. Alex couldn't even blame her.

"I'm sorry I scared you." He turned and headed out of the cave, needing to be alone to collect himself. "I seem to have lost my appetite as well. I'm going for a walk."

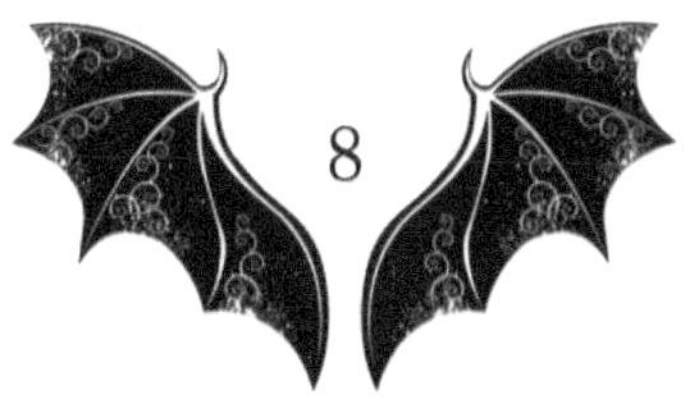

After a lengthy walk to examine the traps, Alex felt more himself. The dragon had gone back to sleep, and he was ready to try again with the princess. He wasn't a monster. Meredith was right; Princess Raelyn would grow accustomed to him. If Alex could just keep his temper in check and the pain at bay long enough to talk to her, surely he could better explain the danger Henry posed and convince her that while he didn't know if what he was doing was the right thing, it was the best choice he could see.

Delivering Princess Raelyn to Henry and Tristan and their stone hearts and possibly some wicked plan to use Raelyn to bully Eynlae would be wrong. Perhaps there wasn't a plot, and Henry merely hoped marrying his son into royalty would make their claim on the throne more secure, but that was simply another way of using the princess for selfish ends. Despite how unkind Raelyn had been to Alex, the idea of sending her to a loveless marriage to a man who just wanted her for her title bothered him.

Besides, he still didn't trust her to keep his secret—especially not after she had so sincerely lied to his face. The thought of Henry sending men into Alex's mountains to hunt them down sent his heart into palpitations and a cold sweat down his back.

Those thoughts were swirling through his head when he reached the edge of the forest before their cave and stopped dead in his tracks, his breath catching.

Princess Raelyn stood in the meadow in front of the cave, wearing a stunning blue dress. The sunlight turned her long braid into spun gold, and a bit of pink colored her upturned face. Her eyes were closed, and she threw her arms wide as a breeze tugged at her skirts. Her soft lips curved into a grin as she laughed. It was a side of her Alex hadn't seen yet—a side that hinted at a personality that embraced joy and felt everything deeply. This Raelyn might tease Lucas or get as excited about the things she enjoyed as Alex did about flying. And his foolish heart was tripping over itself, imagining this beautiful girl laughing like that with him.

Now was a good time to try to start over, while she was in a good mood.

"You have a lovely laugh," Alex said, keeping his voice gentle.

The princess jumped, the blissful expression fleeing her face as her gaze landed on him. His hope dimmed, but she didn't run or even look away. She gazed back at him with determination. Did she want to start over, too? Or perhaps she was trying to manipulate him again.

Watching her closely, he approached her. The nearer he came, the more Princess Raelyn stiffened. Her breaths grew shallower, her face paler, but still, she didn't cower or run, and she kept looking at him even as he stepped into the sunlight in all his cursed dragonman glory. Even when he stopped so close he could have easily touched her golden head, she didn't back away—but he heard her gulp.

"You're afraid," he noted, confused by her conflicting body language.

After a moment, she lifted her chin and declared, "No."

It was probably another lie…or had Jasper and Meredith convinced her to trust him? To test it, he took an exploratory step closer. Her grimace and shiver pricked his heart. He backed away, giving her space, and the stiffness in her shoulders eased.

"You look…" Alex barely stopped himself from saying *gorgeous* as he looked her over again. That might cross a line from gentlemanly to lecherous. Still, wherever Meredith had found that dress, it suited Princess Raelyn well and drew out the blue of her eyes. "Nice," he finished, hoping that was polite and not creepy.

Princess Raelyn flinched back, her gaze finally leaving his face. Apparently any compliments about her appearance were unacceptable.

He tried to smile reassuringly, but she wasn't even looking at him. "We're both going to be miserable if you keep expecting the worst from me."

"There's always the option of helping me get out of the mountains. Then you don't have to be miserable."

If only it were that simple. Unless…was it? Alex stared at the short spring grass around his feet, fighting himself. Maybe he was being paranoid. But no, his reasons were sound, and the princess had lied to him yet again and still saw him as a monster. His secret wouldn't be safe, his family wouldn't be safe—and in the household of a man who had killed his own sister, Raelyn wouldn't be safe, either. But how could he make her understand? She obviously valued duty and loved her family, so if he could win her sympathy for *his* family and persuade her that marrying Tristan wouldn't be the boon for her kingdom that she assumed, perhaps she would change her mind.

The conversation did *not* go as hoped. Alex had envisioned calmly explaining his reasons while Princess Raelyn listened, understanding and empathy filling those sapphire eyes. He'd imagined her beginning to see him as a person who had already lost so much and might lose everything he had left if she said the wrong thing to Henry. That maybe some admiration would steal into her voice, and she would thank him for thinking to protect her and her kingdom from Henry's schemes and Tristan's unfeeling heart.

Instead, the princess called him a liar. She wouldn't listen to his attempted explanations that came out ineloquently and disjointed as the conversation prodded old wounds. Even when he tried to walk away to smother the rising tide of emotions, Raelyn wouldn't let him be, flinging insults at him.

Worries over his family, grief over his parents and old life, anger at Henry, the sting of Raelyn's taunts and disbelief, her inability to see him as anything more than the monster Henry had cursed him to resemble—it all coalesced into a burning coal of fury.

Despite the part of him that didn't want to give into the rage, the dragon's desires became more demanding.

"You're no prince," Raelyn continued ranting, every word hitting him like a whip. "You're not even human!"

Henry's voice cut through Alex's memories as clear as if he were standing right next to him. *Prince? Look at it. It's not even human.* Tears stung his eyes as his whole body shook.

"You're a dragon—"

Alex roared, and the heat of the escaping flames dried his tears on his face. He'd only meant to get the princess to shut up, but he'd made the mistake of giving the dragon a foothold, and it leapt forward to seize his agonized emotions. If he were honest, he was angry enough he didn't want to fight it anymore. Scales sliced through his skin under his clothing. His vision tinged red as he looked back at the offending princess.

"A dragon?" Smoke rolled over his tongue. His muscles seized, and he collapsed to the ground as the transformation passed the point where he had any hope of stopping it. "You're getting a dragon, Princess."

Shaking traveled up his arms, and he pinched his eyes closed until the pain was over and the shift complete. Alex swung his massive head around to look down at the trembling girl. The dragon inside relished her fear, urging him to put an end to the threat to his happiness that she represented. She deserved it for how she had treated him.

"Now I'm a monster, Princess. Now I want to eat you." Almost of its own accord, his tongue flicked toward her.

Alex's human consciousness recoiled in horror at his own words. Had he just said that? Princess Raelyn dropped to her knees, causing the dragon to gloat and hunger.

With a roar, Alex directed the violent fury upward, channeling the dragon fire harmlessly into the sky. *I am in control. I am human, and I'm not hurting her.* He took to the air, desperate to put distance between himself and Raelyn and his family before he said or did anything worse. *No, no, no.*

How had he let the dragon get the better of him twice in two days? Princess Raelyn would never trust him now, and maybe she'd be right not to.

9

A fear that often tormented him after an involuntary shift chased Alex as he flew faster and faster: what if this time, the dragon took over? What if he couldn't shift back, and he lost his mind, that bit of humanity he clung to, and became a blood-thirsty dragon who forgot he had ever been Alexander Tallon? What if this was the time Henry's curse finished its work and stole Alex's very soul?

He landed in a meadow and curled up like a cat, shame gnawing at him as he recalled his own mouth telling a princess whose only crime was cruel words that he wanted to eat her. Jasper had told Alex years ago that just because the dragon put an intrusive idea in his head, that didn't mean Alex had to entertain or act on that thought, nor did he need to feel guilty for having it. A thought couldn't be stopped from bursting into existence, Jasper had said, but once there, it could be either identified as unwanted and re-leased, or embraced and nurtured.

Sometimes Alex caught himself too late and allowed the dragon's rage to have more influence than it deserved. He'd done that too much lately. But Jasper said what mattered was what Alex did when he realized a thought or action was wrong.

The dragon wanted to eat Raelyn. He'd voiced that thought. He shouldn't have.

But I was horrified, and I left. And I owe Raelyn an apology. It was enough to remind him he was still in control and choosing to be a good person, even if his choices were messy and filled with errors. A learning opportunity, Meredith would say. He needed to focus on what he'd done right more than what he'd done wrong, so next time he could do more of the right. Maybe he didn't always live up to his own ideals of kindness and justice, but that didn't mean he was a liar. It only meant that he was fallible and had room to grow.

Monsters didn't experience regret. Demons didn't feel ill because they knew they'd done something wrong. Dragons didn't care if they hurt someone. Alex did. That was enough for him.

But he doubted that would be enough for Princess Raelyn.

Alex sighed and adjusted his massive head, smashing down more grass. He rarely shifted due to the greater danger of being seen, and when he did, he didn't usually land somewhere he would leave a trace. On the rare occasions when he did, he wondered if any humans ever came across gargantuan areas of trampled-down grass and speculated about what had caused it. Possibly, since the others mentioned that the village had rumors that a dragon lived in their mountains. It had terrified them when they first heard the gossip, but nothing had ever come of it.

As Alex focused on the cool breeze on his scales and took deep, slow breaths that made the grass in front of his snout bend back and forth, the dragon silenced. With a groan that was more of a rumble in his chest, he shifted back. The awful pinching, squeezing sensation was over quickly. A breeze brushed over his bare skin, and he curled into a tighter ball, pressing into the lingering heat his dragon form had left on the ground.

How could he apologize to Raelyn? If there was something he could do for her, no matter how difficult—aside from letting her marry Tristan, which he still doubted would end well for the princess or himself—he would do it in a heartbeat. It would be a miracle if she ever liked him now.

A lonely tear slipped from the corner of his eye. It would have been wonderful to have a new friend. A new, gorgeous, female friend…

He mentally burned the thought to ashes. Even if he hadn't completely ruined things with his dragon behavior, what woman would look at his cursed features and find them attractive? A beautiful, sheltered princess raised in a life of luxury would never fall for a smoke-belching exile living in a cave.

Although…Lucas didn't have a problem calling Alex his brother. Jasper had grown up and served in the palace and been the royal steward, and he still bowed his head deferentially to a cursed Alex and said, "my prince." Truthfully, Alex hated when Jasper did that, but if Jasper could respect Alex, maybe Princess Raelyn could see him as more, too. If he could do a better job of controlling the dragon.

He picked at some dirt stuck under his claws. She wouldn't fall in love with him, but maybe they could fall into friendship. That sounded good. Besides, for all her beauty, she *had* been rude, demanding, and a bit arrogant. *Or just frightened and desperate and alone.* Alex hushed himself.

The last thing he needed was to fall hopelessly in love with a girl he barely knew who wouldn't love him back.

Once Alex felt sufficiently calm, he returned to his dragon form—he wasn't about to fly in his human form while naked—and went home. The sun was dipping low toward the horizon as he neared the cave. Jasper was waiting outside, sitting on the boulder near the entrance. Alex smiled when he saw the pile of black fabric and pair of boots next to Jasper.

"Thank you," Alex said as he landed. "It'd be awkward if the princess caught me exposed on top of everything else."

A troubled look entered Jasper's eyes. Alex stilled and inhaled deeply, getting the scent of anxiety rolling off Jasper in waves.

"What is it?"

The wrinkles around Jasper's mouth deepened. "Princess Raelyn isn't here."

54

10

"What do you mean, not here?" Alex demanded.

"She ran into the forest after you left, determined to find her family."

"And you didn't stop her?" The words bellowed out of Alex's mouth, and he winced, trying to control his panic.

Jasper shook his head grimly. "Lucas tried to go after her, but I'm afraid she wouldn't be deterred—"

"He should have dragged her back, if that's what it took," Alex growled. "Foolish, accursed girl!"

His massive dragon claws flexed, digging into the dirt as he looked toward the forest. What if she was hurt? Or worse? What if he'd driven her to her death? It might have been better for Raelyn to risk the dangers of Henry's court than to be torn to pieces by an actual monster.

"And where was Peter? Meredith? How difficult is it to contain one short princess with an injured ankle?"

Raelyn was definitely in trouble. His heart thundered, and his wings twitched as he prepared to take to the sky once more.

"I'm sorry, my prince," Jasper said softly.

Alex huffed, his head drooping. "It's not your fault. I scared her into running. And now I have to find her. Hopefully it isn't already too late."

Without waiting for a reply, he leapt into the air. The trees rushed by beneath him as he flew as quickly as possible while still being able to process the smells from the forest. He'd gotten a good scent on Princess Raelyn after his earlier transformation, and he searched for that scent now. Sometimes he'd catch just a hint of it, but it was fading.

Where are you, Princess?

When he found her, he was going to have to try hard not to shout at her for her stupidity. If she was alive.

If he discovered her mangled corpse, Alex wasn't sure he could ever forgive himself.

The weak traces of Raelyn's scent led him steadily down the mountain. Night was approaching too quickly, and if he didn't find her soon, the chances of finding her unharmed would only get slimmer. Yet again, Alex cursed his own temper and lack of control—and threw in a few curses at the princess's temper, prejudice, and stubbornness, too.

A piercing scream of terror caught him by surprise. His wings jerked, nearly sending him off course. Alex righted himself and sped toward the sound, straining to hear more. He couldn't be too late. He *couldn't.*

Another feminine shriek grated on his ears, but it was closer. Someone shouted something, but he couldn't quite make out what. It had to be coming from near that lake ahead. He locked onto Raelyn's scent as he got closer, but also caught another odor, putrid and strong, that made his jaw clench. *Minotaur.* A growl rumbled in his core as he dove down.

"Bad tasty girl!" a rough, deep voice slurred.

After a moment, another scream rent the air, this one full of pain, not just fear. If that creature had hurt her… Alex roared as he dove toward the shore, catching sight of the minotaur pulling on the princess's leg. As he landed, the beast grabbed her arm and tugged her to her feet. The sharp tang of the princess's terror carried even over the minotaur's stench, and her petite frame shook.

"Give the girl here." Alex let smoke billow from his mouth, intent on intimidating the minotaur into letting Princess Raelyn go without further injury.

Instead, the minotaur pinned her against its filthy, dark fur-covered chest, using her as a shield. Burning orange eyes stared Alex down from the minotaur's bull head. "My dinner! I caught the pretty girl!"

The dragon rankled at the puny minotaur's boldness, and Alex gave a toothy sneer, his anger barely controlled. "I. Don't. Care. She's mine!"

The minotaur glanced over its shoulder, as if considering running. Alex couldn't allow that—it would be difficult for him to follow them into the forest before the princess was hurt or killed. So Alex took a gamble.

"Let her go, or I will roast and eat you both!" He let a bit of dragon fire bubble up but didn't release it.

Alex had always thought minotaurs rather stupid, but this one shook its head and started backing toward the forest, still using Raelyn as a human shield. "You burn me anyway!"

Alex roared his fire into the sky, his frustration mounting. "Give her to me or die." He moved his head forward, testing the air with his tongue to see if the dragon would be able to discern the minotaur's intent, but it was difficult to catch much other than the minotaur's and Raelyn's combined fear.

After a moment's hesitation, the minotaur threw the princess at Alex, then sprinted into the trees. The dragon inside was eager to tear the troublesome monster apart, but Alex's gaze caught on Princess Raelyn as she curled into a ball on the grass. The minotaur disappeared into the woods and the dragon thrashed, but the sound of crying filled his ears. Alex's heart softened. All thoughts of berating her for running away vanished like smoke on the wind. She'd already been through enough—too much, in fact.

With a deep breath, Alex quieted the dragon and reached for his humanity, wincing as his body contracted back into his cursed human form. He approached the sobbing princess—careful to use his wings to cover himself for the princess's sake. She was still curled up, as if she could make herself small enough to escape his notice.

"Princess?" he asked tentatively. "It's over. You can get up."

To his relief, she untucked her head. Bleary, tear-filled blue eyes stared up at him from a pale face.

"Are you all right?" He thought he smelled blood, but it could have been the taint of the minotaur.

The only response she gave him was a sob. *Stupid, Alex.* She was separated from her family, and a dragon and a minotaur had threatened to eat her; of course she wasn't all right.

"Are you hurt?" he tried again.

The princess shifted, wariness in her expression. "Not badly."

If only he'd brought Meredith along. She would know how to put the princess at ease. What would Meredith do? Alex cautiously reached out to give Princess Raelyn a reassuring pat on her shoulder, but the moment his hand touched her, she flinched. *Meredith doesn't have claws,* he reminded himself with a grimace.

"I'm not going to hurt you," he promised, hoping that by some miracle, she would believe him.

Her nod bolstered his hope, but then she broke down into a worse fit of choking sobs than before, returning to her curled-up position. With a flash, Alex saw himself—nine years old, terrified of his own new monstrous form, his heart still raw over the loss of his parents and shattered by his uncle's betrayal, confused and unsure he could even trust the servants who had helped him escape. The first night he'd been too exhausted to think, but the second, he'd curled up in a very similar fashion under a blanket in the shadows at the edge of a cave and wept so hard he'd felt like he'd never be able to stop. Princess Raelyn was alone, without her family, afraid, unsure who to trust, and had nearly died more than once recently. No wonder her weeping so closely echoed his own past tears.

And he bore much of the blame for her distress.

Alex crumbled under the realization and knelt next to her, desperately wishing he could take away her fear and anguish. "Oh, Princess." The words came out in a rushed whisper. "I'm sorry. I'm so sorry."

Much like Meredith had done to him many times over the last twelve years, Alex lightly stroked Princess Raelyn's hair. If she hadn't been crying, he might have gotten distracted by the soft strands beneath his fingers, but he focused on comforting the girl he'd so badly wronged, even if unintentionally. "You're safe."

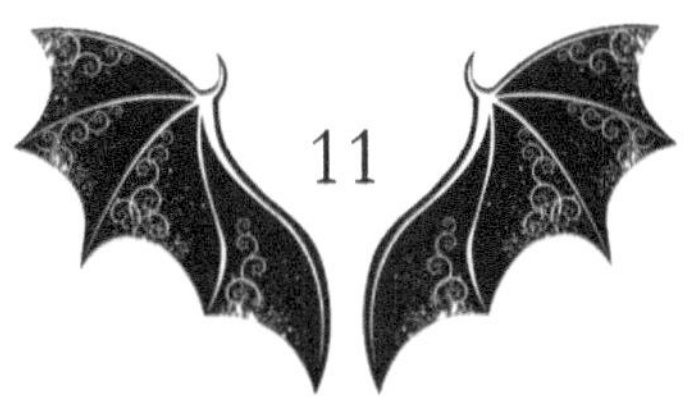

11

The tension eased from the princess's body and her sobs quieted as Alex continued stroking her hair. When she steadied herself and lifted her head, he dropped his hand to rub her upper back instead. Now that she was more aware of her surroundings, would she be all right with him being there? With him touching her?

It was inappropriate given the circumstances, but his heart did a little leap when she didn't move away from him, just closed her eyes and breathed deeply. Maybe she was in shock, but at least she didn't completely hate or distrust him. He took it as a sign there was a path forward toward friendship despite their fight.

On the subject of keeping things in check, he needed to stop touching Raelyn before the urge to embrace her grew any stronger. He doubted she'd appreciate it if he wrapped his arms around her and pulled her close, even in a gesture of comfort. Especially since, he remembered with some chagrin, he was naked.

So Alex reluctantly stood, keeping his wings uncomfortably crossed over himself. "Do you want to come with me back to the cave?" he asked, hoping this wouldn't devolve into another argument about taking her to her family.

The look she gave him was pure confusion. "You... Why?"

Now it was Alex's turn to be confused. "So you don't get eaten?"

The princess kept watching him. It might have been the longest she'd ever done so. "Why do you care? Why would you help me after what I said?" Finally, she looked away, but something about the movement seemed more weary than frightened. "Why did you save me? You said you wouldn't."

He regretted saying that, even if he had only said it in an attempt to squash her ideas of running. "Would you have preferred I let you get eaten? You needed help."

"But after everything I said?" Raelyn sat up and drew her legs up to her chest. "I was—"

"I told you I prefer rude honesty to flattering lies," Alex said with a sigh. "I suppose I was asking for it."

"No."

Her disagreement caught him by surprise. But he could see her gathering her courage, so he stayed quiet, hardly daring to breathe as he waited to hear what she would say. An excuse? Or an apology?

"I was unnecessarily cruel," the princess said, her tone heavy.

It wasn't an apology, but the fact she was humble enough to admit wrongdoing encouraged him. Even as night fell around them, Alex felt like he'd seen a spot of light, and he wanted to seize it.

He sat down, absently adjusting his wings to accommodate the position, and barely remembered to keep one wing tucked over his lower body. What should he say? Perhaps some reassurance he wasn't the kind of person who repaid an offense with a graver offense. At least, he tried not to be.

"What now, then?" he said slowly. "You were cruel. So I should let you die? Or eat you myself?"

Even in the dark, he saw how her entire body went rigid.

"I'm not going to, by the way," he said before she could start yelling at him again. He tapped his claws against the grass. "Twelve years I've been like this. I haven't eaten anyone yet; I don't intend to start now." *If I did, I wouldn't start with a princess. Probably would be too tender and set my expectations all wrong.* A chuckle accompanied the thought, and he eyed the princess, remembering how she'd laughed standing in the sun. Perhaps underneath all that prejudice, she was hiding a sense of humor.

"Besides," Alex said, fighting a smile, "if I started with royalty, I imagine no one else would taste as good."

The scowl she sent his way was unconvincing. "That's not funny," she protested, but there wasn't any vehemence behind the words.

Her ability to take a joke pleased him, and the lighter attitude did seem to help ease some of her fears, so he kept going.

"All right," he said, fighting another chuckle, "maybe it was in poor...taste."

Princess Raelyn looked away with a harrumph that didn't match her sagging posture. The next words that left her lips killed his jovial mood. "You made it sound like you were going to eat me."

Alex had been too desperate to consider how she would interpret his words. He grunted, slightly annoyed she couldn't just accept that he'd saved her. "I don't think the minotaur would have understood, 'this girl is not for eating.' They're not particularly bright." *And you're not being particularly bright, Alex, getting defensive after you hurt someone.* "I am sorry, though. I also shouldn't have lost my temper or threatened you. And I'm sorry that because of that you thought I was scaring off the minotaur so I could eat you myself. I can't help if you're afraid of how I look. But you shouldn't have to fear how I act."

He had to force the words past his tight throat, resolving yet again to do a better job of fighting the dragon. So far as he could help it, he wouldn't threaten or terrorize Princess Raelyn. No matter what horrible things she might say, he didn't want to be the reason she curled into a ball and wept ever again.

She lifted her face toward the sky. "I don't understand."

Alex tilted his head, both confused and amused. "The concept of an apology?" he asked. That *would* explain the princess's behavior.

"I don't understand why you're being nice."

Nice. She'd called him nice. Alex's internal celebration might have become an external dance or punching of the air, except that Raelyn looked over at him.

"You were angry, and you had a right to be. And after what I said…don't you hate me?"

He sobered, taking a moment to sort through his feelings and consider what was safe to say. Her words had cut him deeply, and even though he wanted to move forward, he couldn't deny that he was wary of her sharp tongue.

"I don't particularly like you right now," he admitted. "But I'm not sure that's entirely your fault. I've been…harsh toward you. Because you remind me of everything that's been taken from me." An involuntary growl escaped, and he cleared his throat, embarrassed, and focused on the princess. "I know it can't be easy to believe everything I've told you because I haven't earned your trust. I'm not trying to be monstrous by keeping you, but I don't know how to convince you I'm telling the truth. And then…" He bowed his head, his stomach twisting in on itself. "I kind of proved your accusations correct. I was…monstrous."

Princess Raelyn shivered. It was freezing by the lake now that it was dark. Even with his dragon heat building to counteract the cold— or perhaps because it—with every passing moment he wanted more and more to be back in his room in front of a fire. But he knew he couldn't rush her. Winning any measure of understanding or trust from this young woman was going to take patience.

"No," Raelyn said quietly, interrupting his thoughts of his cozy room. "I'm sorry."

Alex started. Her forehead rested on her knees, so she couldn't see his jaw hanging open.

"The things I said…I was frightened and angry, and…I don't know if I believe you. But I shouldn't have been so cruel." She opened her eyes and Alex slammed his mouth closed.

She sounded sincere, but she'd lied to him multiple times already. He wished he were in dragon form so he'd be able to sense her honesty without touching her, but if he'd been a dragon still, he had a feeling she would have been too frightened and defensive to apologize. Regardless, her apology strengthened Alex's belief that his instincts were right—she wasn't merely a condescending princess.

But while she had been wrong, she wasn't responsible for his reaction.

"I'm sorry I scared you into running," he said.

They talked for a while longer, Alex trying again to explain the complexity of wanting to help her but being unwilling to deliver her to marry an unjustly crowned prince in the court of a murderer. In the end, he wasn't sure he'd convinced her, but she agreed to give him another chance—and asked him to give her another chance to be less rude as well.

"Second chances all around," Alex agreed. At least they could go home.

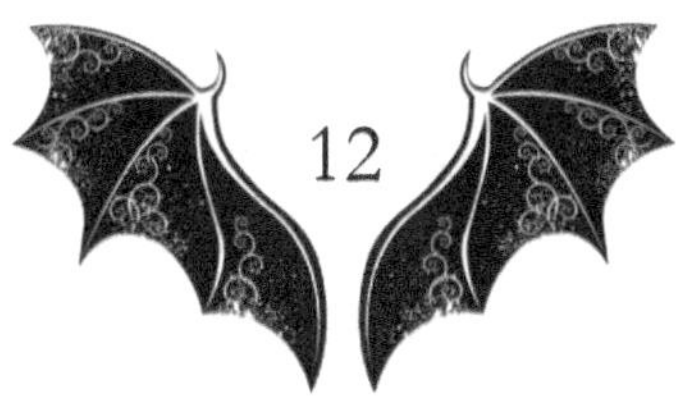

12

Alex stood, his wings still carefully positioned for modesty's sake. He was growing anxious to return home, warm his cold wings and toes, and put food in his gnawing stomach. "Ready to go back?"

"The cave is better than here," the princess said as she also stood.

Alex heartily agreed, but there was the small problem of getting there. Or more precisely, getting the princess there. He cleared his throat, hoping she couldn't see him blushing in the dark. "This is awkward, but…I'm naked."

Princess Raelyn replied without missing a beat, "I noticed."

Alex couldn't help the smirk that twisted his lips, especially when Raelyn started stammering, as if realizing how brazen that had sounded. Maybe he was wrong and there *was* a chance for something more than just friendship…probably far in the future, but still.

He laughed, interrupting her stuttering. "Sorry to make you uncomfortable." Sort of. At least now he knew that she'd noticed he was a man, too, beneath the horns. "Unfortunate side effect of shifting," he explained as he backed up to give himself sufficient room. "But I don't want to walk all the way back naked. Between trying to stay decent and the branches, it would be a long and miserable walk." And he absolutely couldn't carry her in the manner he had the night he first found her. "So brace yourself, Princess."

The familiar burning, straining sensation torn through his muscles as he forced himself to shift. His senses and awareness heightened in his dragon form. If he listened closely, he could even hear Raelyn's heartbeat speed up. Despite their progress, it was too much to hope the sight of him in dragon form wouldn't frighten her. He knelt down and drew back his wings to give her access so she could clamber onto his back. It had been a long time since he'd last done this with Lucas.

"Climb on," he said when Raelyn didn't seem to catch on to his intention.

The princess jumped. "What?"

"It's that or I pick you up with my paws and carry you."

She continued to stand there, staring at him like he'd lost his mind.

"Choose quickly, Princess. I'm growing impatient." His dragon form provided more heat, but at the cost of weakening the wall between Alex's will and the dragon's emotions. It also came with a bigger stomach, which made his hunger more acute. Not to mention the others were going to be worried sick.

"All right," Princess Raelyn murmured. Her steps were hesitant as she approached, and her wide eyes locked on his mouth.

Right, the eating thing. Alex turned his head away and hoped she'd hurry up. A hand brushed his leg, and then he felt her scrabbling over his scales. A light weight settled at the base of his neck. *Finally.*

"There's nothing to hold on to!" The princess's high-pitched protest grated in his ears.

"Better hold tight with your legs, then." Without giving her a chance to reconsider, he flapped his wings and flew into the night. Time to go home. Home for him, at least.

They'd been flying for a few minutes, Alex mulling over his chances of getting to eat supper before Jasper, Meredith, and Peter sat him down for a lecture, when a strange sound pulled him out of his thoughts. The quiet noise stopped abruptly, and Alex thought he must have imagined it.

But then another sound came from behind his head, this time louder, uninhibited.

The princess was laughing. He glanced backward and caught a brief glimpse of her on his back, her arms flung out and head thrown back as she laughed like she hadn't a care in the world. She…liked flying.

Alex grinned and banked hard to the side as they approached the cave, careful not to cause her to fall, but enough to give her a taste of more daring flight. The laughter stopped, but there was no gasp or other indication that she was upset. He landed in the clearing in front of the cave and knelt to make it easier for her to dismount.

Her boots and hands slid down his leg, and more giggles erupted from Raelyn. Alex craned his head to look back at her, surprised and amused. Her eyes were bright above a childlike smile. If she could be like this all the time, she'd fit right in.

"Enjoying yourself, Princess?"

The slight pink on her cheeks deepened to crimson. "Sorry."

"Don't apologize." Alex smiled, mind already whirring over ideas of how to use their shared love of flying to bond. "There's no sensation quite like flying."

He cooled the dragon and focused on his humanity, fighting a groan as his body pinched and shrank.

"Alex!" Meredith hurried out of the cave, torch in one hand and black fabric in the other. "Are you all right?"

He tried to answer, but a moan came out instead. The shift completed, leaving him kneeling on his hands and knees. He took a moment to collect himself before standing.

"Yes. Found the princess." He nodded toward Raelyn, who had

turned her back on him. *Don't want to see me naked again, Princess?* He fought a smirk.

"I can see that," Meredith snapped. Alex winced. Meredith was *not* happy, and he wasn't entirely sure who her ire was directed at. She handed him a pair of trousers, but her scowl was focused on Raelyn's back. "I'm unsure if I'm relieved she's in one piece or disappointed."

Alex stepped into the trousers and stuck the end of his tail through the extra hole in the back. He should have realized Meredith would be prickly about keeping Raelyn around after the things she'd said. Alex often thought Meredith cared more about his feelings than he did. But he was just starting to make progress with the princess, and he wasn't about to let Meredith mess that up.

He clicked his tongue as he buttoned up his trousers. "Now, Meredith. Be nice to my guest."

Meredith looked at him, eyebrows raised. "What, she came back willingly?"

"I suspect it had more to do with not wanting to get eaten, but yes. I'm decent, by the way, Princess. You can turn around."

Raelyn's shoulders hunched as she peered over at him. "I think we may have different definitions of decent," she said, turning to face them.

Alex snickered, noting how the princess was very obviously avoiding looking at his bare chest. He sometimes wondered when looking in a mirror if he were handsome. He liked to think he was, but how was he to know? Once, he'd even awkwardly asked Meredith. She'd burst out laughing and told him he'd have been a real heartbreaker at court. Did the princess think so, too?

These thoughts weren't productive, so he seized a different topic. "Turns out the princess likes flying. She was laughing like an exuberant child." Maybe his hunger made him stupid, or maybe the idea of the princess finding the human parts of him attractive made him daring, but his teasing side took over. "She's actually kind of cute when she's not being rude."

To his immense satisfaction, Princess Raelyn's moonlit face turned red again as she muttered incoherently. He turned to Meredith. "We've agreed to give each other another chance at being polite. Maybe we'll even reach friendly. If not"—he forced his expression neutral as he glanced over at Raelyn—"I can always eat her."

Meredith's palm impacted his shoulder in a slap that left his skin stinging. She glared at him, a warning look in her eyes. "Alexander!"

"Ow!" He played it up, rubbing his shoulder and giving Meredith a mournful expression. "All right, all right." Turning back to Raelyn, he said, "Sorry. I'll stop with the jokes about eating you."

Raelyn's stiff posture relaxed, but she still watched him through narrowed eyes as she murmured, "Thanks."

They went into the cave, Meredith taking Raelyn to borrow another clean dress. Alex, meanwhile, headed to Jasper's room to ask Lucas for help with putting on a shirt before supper.

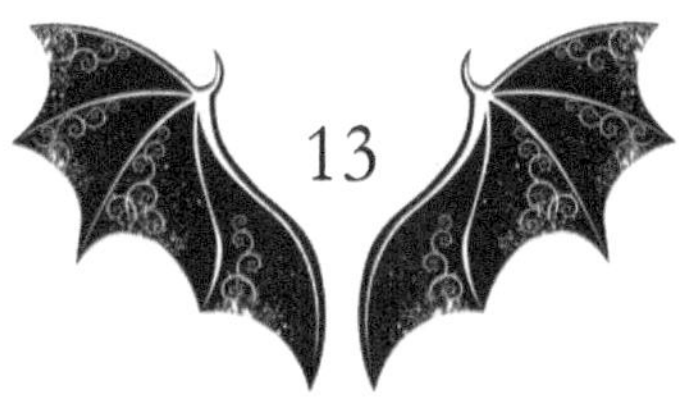

13

Alex knocked on Jasper's door, and moments later, the door was forcefully thrown open by a wide-eyed Lucas.

"Is Alex—Alex!" Lucas barreled forward, slamming into Alex's chest so hard he rocked backward a step, his tail moving to help him maintain his balance against Lucas's forceful hug. His friend's hands were cold where they clapped against his skin. "You're back. You're all right and you're home."

The light from the fireplace illuminated Jasper's room, including a small table and chair that had been shoved into the corner to make room for the mess of blankets and pillows on the floor that was Lucas's temporary bed. Jasper sat on his bed leaning against a pile of cushions, and he smiled over the book in his hands. "Did you find Princess Raelyn?"

Alex nodded as he patted Lucas's back. "Yes. She's with Meredith getting changed into something less dirty before supper. A minotaur sort of dragged her through the mud."

"A what?" Lucas finally released him. "Is she all right?"

"She was understandably shaken, but I think she's all right." Alex smirked. "You should have heard her laughing with glee on the flight home."

Jasper lifted his eyebrows. "Flight?"

"On my back in dragon form." Alex rolled his eyes. "I didn't carry a princess in a state of undress, and I kept myself covered while in human form. Your sense of propriety can rest easy."

Jasper made a humming sound, but Alex thought he caught a twitch of a smile from the old man.

"I could use your help with my shirt, Lucas." Alex winked at Jasper. "Will also give you a few minutes to yourself."

Jasper snorted. "Maybe I'll actually get some reading accomplished."

"You probably have that old thing memorized anyway, Jasper," Lucas said with an exaggerated shake of his head.

"Always more to glean from Lantus the Wise, young one."

Lucas screwed up his nose, and Alex's mouth twisted around a suppressed laugh. Alex hooked his arm behind Lucas's neck and pulled him out of the room, closing the door after him.

"I can't see, you oversized bat." Lucas shoved Alex's arm off his shoulders and ducked back into Jasper's room to grab a candle. "All right, now we can go."

Alex tried to frown but had the feeling it wasn't very convincing. "The dragon is offended."

"The dragon can grow up." Lucas stuck out his tongue and headed down the tunnel. "So did it take you a long time to find her, or was it hard to get her to come back? She's really not hurt or anything? Did she yell at you again? Was she even going the right way? Do you think she could have made it? Is she angry to be here still? Oh, what did Mom say? She was so upset with the princess—"

"Slow down." Alex shook his head. He'd never understood where Lucas got all his questions and endless stream of words. Sometimes it drove him near insane, but at the same time, Lucas's constant chatter was comforting. It was home. "I found her fairly quickly, thankfully, since she was seconds away from being eaten by a minotaur." His stomach twisted a little at the thought.

"Oh." Lucas's pace slowed as they turned into the dining room.

"She's all right, though?"

"I think so. Mostly, at least."

A clatter came from the kitchen as they passed by, and Alex glanced over. Peter was busy at the fireplace, heating something up.

"Hold on." Alex turned aside and added some wood to the low-burning fire by the dining table, stoking the flames up to a roar. "Ah." He closed his eyes and breathed in the soft smell of wood smoke, enjoying the heat against his skin.

"So was she happy to see you, then, since you saved her?" Lucas prodded.

Alex stood with a sigh and turned in the direction of his room at the far end of the cave. "Not really, no. I kind of threatened to roast her and the minotaur to scare the minotaur into releasing her, and…she thought the dragon—she thought I was going to eat her."

"Oh." Lucas bit his lower lip. "But…then…did you force her to return? Will she try to run away again?"

"No, she agreed to come with me after we talked, and I apologized. Actually, we both apologized. And I hope she won't run again, but…I honestly don't know." He was determined to make this work and win her over, but would determination be enough?

Lucas gawked at him as they walked side by side down the tunnel to Alex's room. "She apologized? So she's going to be nicer? She…doesn't seem very nice. Well, sometimes she seems all right, but she's mean to you, and you're the best. I don't know what she said to you, but it must have been terrible for you to get so angry, and I hate that. I hate that she was cruel to you—"

"Whoa, Lucas!" Alex stopped in front of his door and put his hands on Lucas's shoulders. The lad was getting close to being as tall as Alex was, and Alex was still having trouble adjusting. "Yes, she said some awful things. But she apologized, and I don't think she really meant everything she said. We're going to give her another chance, and that means no hating, right? What does Jasper always say?"

Lucas fixated on the candle in his hand. "Hearts full of hate forget how to love."

Alex nodded and entered his room. Unsurprisingly, it was dark and colder than he liked since he hadn't been in it all day. He longed to get the fire going, but he was also starving and would be leaving the room soon, anyway, so he went to his dresser and plucked a shirt from the stack of black clothing.

"So the others were angry with Princess Raelyn?" Alex queried as he pulled the shirt over his head.

Lucas set the candle down on Alex's bookshelf with a shrug. "Mostly Mom. You know how protective she is. And she didn't like that when I tried to stop the princess…" He rubbed the back of his neck. "Never mind. Turn around so I can see the buttons in the candlelight."

But Alex didn't turn. "Jasper mentioned you tried to stop her. What happened?"

Lucas shifted, staring at the floor. "I know I should have tried harder. I ran after her and called for her to come back, but she screamed at me not to lay a finger on her. She was furious, Alex. It scared me…just a little. And I was angry with her for whatever she said to upset you." He ducked his head, hiding his face. "Not to mention she's a *princess,* and she gave a direct order… I didn't know what to do, so I stopped chasing her."

Lucas gripped the hem of his tunic and twisted it while his foot tapped an anxious rhythm against the stone. "I thought maybe she'd realize she was being foolish and come back, or that you'd return and stop her." His shoulders bunched up to his ears. "She didn't return, and neither did you, but by then Mom and Dad wouldn't let me go looking for her, and I wouldn't have known where to start, anyway; I'm not as good at tracking as you. But I was so worried, and you were right, she's just a girl with a hurt ankle and all she did was yell. I should have dragged her back, even though she would have been angry at me. I'm sorry, Alex…" He sniffled.

"Lucas—"

"I knew you wanted her to stay here, and I knew it was dangerous for her to be alone in the forest, but I just watched her run away because she yelled. I let you down, and I'm really sorry. If she had been eaten and I could have saved her, it would have been my—"

"Whoa, no, Lucas, stop." Alex lifted Lucas's chin with the side of his finger until Lucas met his eyes. "You didn't let me down. She isn't your responsibility; she's mine. Thank you for trying, but you're worth so much more to me than some random princess." He smiled sadly. "That's why she's still here. To prevent Henry from learning where we are, so you all stay safe."

"And to keep her safe because Henry's a snake," Lucas said. "Right?"

Alex nodded. "Are you good?"

"Yes." Lucas brushed a tear from his cheek with the heel of his hand. "I'm glad you're not mad at me."

"Oh, give me time. I'm sure you'll do something to annoy me and give me an excuse to drop you in a lake."

Lucas laughed. "I'd love to go swimming but seeing as I might freeze to death if you dropped me in a lake right now, I suppose I'll have to behave."

"Behave?" Alex feigned a shocked gasp. "Do you know how to do that?"

"Better than you, apparently." Lucas grabbed Alex's shoulder and forced him to turn around so he could button up the shirt under Alex's wings. "I haven't ruined any clothes recently, and I haven't threatened to eat any girls."

Alex twisted around to try to see Lucas. "Why you—"

"Hold still, Your Highness." Teasing amusement laced Lucas's words.

Every once in a while, one of the others would call Alex *Your Highness* or *my prince*. Lucas was the only one that Alex didn't mind when he did it, because Lucas only did so in teasing, usually when he thought Alex was being overdramatic or needy. There were no expectations or hopes behind it that Alex could never live up to when Lucas said it, just affection.

"Done." Lucas grabbed the candle and jumped over Alex's tail as he moved around between Alex and the door. "I already ate, but can I sit with you for supper?"

Alex snorted as he shooed Lucas out of the room, and they headed back toward the dining room. "So you can talk the princess's ear off? I think not."

"Aw, but—"

"We're just trying to get to know each other again," Alex said. "I need some time alone with Princess Raelyn to start over."

"Fine. I suppose that makes sense. I just was hoping I didn't have to go back to spending time with Jasper. If the princess is staying, we need to make a new room. For her or for me, I don't care, but Jasper snores and he's so boring, and he keeps telling me to sit still and stop fidgeting. I hate sitting still!"

"Oh, I'm aware." Alex chuckled. "Very well. We'll look into adapting another cave into a new room for you. Now get out of here. I have a princess to entertain."

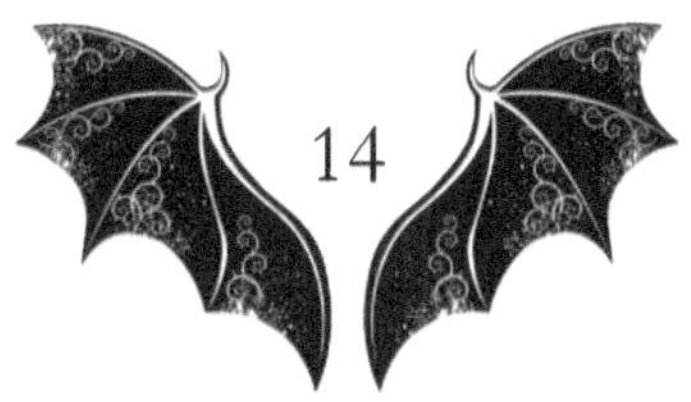

14

Although the princess wasn't hostile at supper, she wasn't relaxed, either. When Alex asked her what stories she'd heard about him, and she was too frightened and embarrassed to answer, he finally understood her tension. He couldn't have known before talking to her that her opinion was already poisoned against him, but it made his actions—and particularly his abrupt announcement they had once been betrothed—look far more beastly than he had realized.

As they finished their meal in silence, she kept acting like she was about to speak. Alex would perk up, eager for her to just *talk* to him, but then she would shrink back in her chair without a word. He ate the last bite of his food and studied her across the table. Her braid was a mess from her tangle with the minotaur, and there was some dirt smudged on her temple that was at odds with the clean dress she'd borrowed from Meredith. The dress was a touch loose on her, but Alex thought she looked striking in the dark green.

Raelyn finally lifted her eyes from her empty plate and Alex sat a little straighter. She was looking at him. *Right* at him, without flinching.

"Can… If… That is, I…" She trailed off and ducked her head, averting her gaze.

Alex's heart fell, but he kept his tone nonchalant and slightly teasing as he attempted to coax out the brave side of her again. "Spit it out, Princess. I promise not to turn into a dragon." He winked, but she wasn't even looking.

"I need to know if my family is all right," the princess said as she traced the goblet's rim with a slender finger. She met his eyes, and Alex scarcely breathed. "Can you look for them? We were near the top of the Thet…the Gonah Way when the manticore attacked. I need to know if they survived. If my parents and brother are…alive." He would have heard the tremor in her voice even without his sensitive hearing. "They're probably fine and long gone, but I need to know for certain. If…if there are bodies on the pass."

Alex mentally cursed himself. How could he have been so blind and selfish? All this time thinking about protecting his own family, assuming Raelyn's family had to have survived the manticore attack, but not considering that if he were in Raelyn's shoes, he would also be sick with worry and want reassurance. He shoved away from the table and stood. He couldn't let her go and could never truly make up for everything he had done already, but at least he could make this one thing right. Even if it would be dangerous and Jasper and Meredith would disapprove. The princess deserved that much.

"I had to ask," Raelyn whispered. Her head was bowed, but the firelight glinted on wetness under her eyes. Would he ever stop making her cry?

"You shouldn't have needed to ask," he answered honestly as he strode in the direction of the cave entrance. Thankfully Meredith didn't have a dragon's hearing, and from her place by the entry to the dining room, she must not have heard Raelyn's request because she merely smiled at him and nodded as he passed. She probably assumed he wanted to go for an evening stroll to relax. Alex didn't tell her otherwise—he wasn't in the mood for an argument.

Storm clouds were gathering as Alex took to the sky. The air didn't smell like rain yet, but Peter might have been right about a storm coming. Just as well, as the clouds would help hide him from unwanted attention. He made for the highest point on the pass between Eynlae and Rethalyon, recalling what Raelyn had said. It took a while to get there, especially since he slowed down and flew close to the treetops as he drew closer, but he couldn't risk being seen.

No one was at the trail's apex, but the faint reek of blood lingered on the road a little further downhill to the east. It was old, without much to tell Alex, but there were no bodies, and he didn't see anything that looked like graves. Although the Eynlaeans would probably try to transport a fallen royal's body back home. He couldn't return to Princess Raelyn with the news that he'd found nothing and hoped that meant everything was fine. That answer wouldn't satisfy him if it were his own family. But would they have headed to Eynlae or gone onward to Rethalyon?

After a moment of debate, he flew above the pass, heading away from Eynlae. To his relief, it didn't take long to start smelling smoke, then to catch sight of the smoke, and then to pick up on the scents of human and horse and the sound of quiet chatter. He got as close as he dared to the campsite before landing. It was risky, but he'd have to get near enough to see—or at least to overhear. Unfortunately, he had no idea what Raelyn's parents or brother looked like. Perhaps he should have asked before flying off like a fool.

Alex was so busy chiding himself that he almost walked right out in front of a man sitting on a boulder in a small clearing well outside of the camp. As quickly as he could manage, Alex tiptoed backward, careful not to hit his wings, tail, or horn against anything. He sank down behind a bush and waited for his heart to slow back down. *Definitely not telling the others how close of a call that was.*

Peering around the side of the bush, he kept low and only let his right eye peek out. The man hadn't moved, just sat there holding his head in his hands. Strange. It looked like… Mourning, Alex realized. It looked like a broken man in mourning. Could it be Gareth, Raelyn's brother? Or maybe her father? His hair was a light brown, not a bright gold like Raelyn's. Was it better to wait and see what the man did, or sneak around to try to eavesdrop on the camp? Alex's gaze caught on the bandage wrapped around the man's upper arm. This might be only a knight who had been injured in the fight against the minotaur. Alex's time would be better spent elsewhere—

The crunch of footsteps sounded, approaching from the camp, and Alex ducked back behind the bush. He pushed aside some leaves and managed a partially obstructed view of the man as he jumped up and spun toward the newcomer. The mourner's right hand grabbed for a sword he wasn't wearing. Almost certainly a knight, if his first instinct when interrupted was to reach for his sword. The man from the camp carried a torch, and although no gray had yet touched his brown hair, he appeared to be middle-aged. Alex started to ease his hands out of the bush, but froze at the older man's hard voice.

"Gareth."

It *was* Prince Gareth? Alex squinted at the young man, recalling that Raelyn *had* said her brother would kill him. Princes were trained as knights as well, so he should have realized her brother would have a knight's reflexes. *Full of idiocy tonight, aren't you, Alexander?*

"I've discussed it with Sir Christopher," the older man said, his tone heavy with authority. It had to be King Weston, Raelyn's father. "Every day she's missing, our chances of finding her alive dwindle. We aren't going to find her, and we can't afford to waste more time when King Henry expected us to have already arrived."

"It's not wasting time!" Gareth's clenched fists and angry shout had Alex reconsidering his belief that the stern man was the king. "I'm not abandoning her!"

"It's not abandoning." In the torchlight, the older man's expression remained stiff. "I don't want to admit it, either, but she's gone, son, and searching—"

"No!" Gareth protested. "We haven't found her body!"

Alex ducked his head at the desperation in Gareth's tone. Not only had he not considered that Raelyn would still be worrying about her family's safety, he'd hardly spared more than a thought about the extent of her family's hurt. So much hurt, in fact, that Prince Gareth was yelling at his own father and king.

"That doesn't mean she's alive." King Weston's words were taut in a way that told Alex he was barely containing his own emotions. "Her body could have been taken far—"

"How could you *say* that?" Gareth backed away from his father, apparently not picking up on the king's pain. "She's your daughter! She's counting on us!"

"Eynlae is counting on us. We must go to Rethalyon—"

"Because the treaty has always been more important than Raelyn," Gareth spat.

Eavesdropping on this conversation might have been a terrible mistake. Not just because of how guilty it was making Alex feel, but because if he were in Gareth's place, he'd be horrified to know that a stranger was listening in on his heartache-fueled temper tantrum.

"Hasn't it?" Gareth was still shouting. "Do you even love her?"

"Of course I love her!" The torch in King Weston's trembling hand cast juddering flickers over his tortured expression. "I loved her. I hope she knew that."

With as worried as Raelyn was about her family, Alex was certain she knew her father loved her, and certain that she loved him in return. But because of Alex, Weston might wonder for the rest of his life. *Maybe I was wrong. Maybe I should bring her back.*

"Then don't give up on her!" Gareth begged. "Keep looking—"

"I have a duty to my people to fulfill." The heaviness in Weston's declaration settled like a weight on Alex's shoulders. He'd put Raelyn's father in a horrible situation where he had to make hard decisions as a king first and father second, and the guilt was staggering.

"And I have a duty to my sister!" Gareth made Raelyn's temper and stubbornness look tame. "Let me stay with a couple knights and—"

"No."

"Alone then!"

"So I can lose another child?" Weston demanded. The agony in his eyes felt like a blow to Alex's chest. "Absolutely not. We leave for the Rethali palace in the morning. All of us. This is not a discussion, Gareth. This is an order."

Gareth turned away from Weston with a growl and scooped up a stone. Alex's breath caught, his blood heating in response to his fear as Gareth lobbed the stone in his direction. Had the prince spotted him? But the stone crashed through the woods off to Alex's right, and Gareth turned back toward the king.

"Hang your orders! Hang King Henry and his stupid son! She's my sister, my *best friend*, and I won't leave her to the mercy of some monster! People don't just vanish without a trace! Something took her—"

"Enough!" Weston bellowed. "I want her back as much as you do—"

"Yes. So you can make your payment to Rethalyon for your port and trading privileges." Gareth's words struck out like a viper.

Alex cringed. He'd been blinded by hurt himself before and knew how easy it could be to lash out at people who cared about him because he felt powerless, but couldn't Gareth see how much his father loved him? That he only wanted to protect his son and was also carrying the weight of inexpressible sorrow? *If my parents were still here, I would never…* But they weren't. They were gone, and the chasm their loss had left inside him yawned back open now as he confronted Prince Gareth and King Weston's sorrow.

"If you hadn't signed Raelyn away like some—some breeding mare, she wouldn't be in danger," Gareth ranted. "She'd be home, flirting with a nice Eynlaean boy, not missing in the mountains, probably being tormented by some beast!"

The words stung like a physical slap. Alex hadn't *meant* to torment her, but he had.

"You will hold your tongue, Prince Gareth." The king's tone suggested that whatever line they had in their complicated relationship as father and son and king and prince, Gareth had finally crossed it. "I thought you had matured past this."

"If you don't let me keep looking, I will *never* forgive you!"

Alex let the branches ease back into place and sat down, hanging his head. His stomach writhed, and dragon heat twisted in his core. Maybe he should fly home, get Raelyn, and take her to her family. It seemed so much simpler to keep Princess Raelyn when he didn't dwell on the bereavement her family was experiencing. A pain he understood too well.

But it didn't change that his parents were dead because of Henry—because of the father of the man Raelyn was supposed to marry. There was still the chance Henry would hurt or use her, or that Tristan would be as heartless as his father. And if Alex returned Raelyn to her family, he wasn't certain she wouldn't immediately recount her time with him and give Gareth his monster to hunt. Especially when it seemed likely Gareth would ask her questions until he learned the truth and was eager for a fight. And if Alex evaded Gareth, then Henry would find out, and Alex and his family might never be safe again.

There was no option where someone wasn't in danger. No choice where Alex could be positive that everyone was guaranteed to not get hurt. He empathized with King Weston, caught in a situation where any choice felt like a betrayal.

"Return to camp," Raelyn's father ordered, but he sounded more exhausted than upset.

"Not until you agree to keep looking."

"She's dead, Gareth! Don't you get that? She's dead!" The sob that broke through Weston's words pounded at Alex, making his head ache. Or maybe that was the sympathetic tears that he refused to let fall as he relived how shattered he'd been after his parents' deaths.

"It's Raelyn, Father. She's my sister, my *only* sister. I can't give up. I refuse!"

In the silence that followed, Alex drew his knees up to his chest. His tail curled over his feet. He needed to keep it together. If he made too much sound, he'd draw their attention, and in Gareth's current mood, not having a sword might not stop him from killing anything that looked remotely like a monster. The thought of being attacked sent a stab of fear through him, and the dragon stirred in response. *No.* He breathed out slowly, forcing the dragon down.

"All right," King Weston finally said. "A compromise. One more day. We look for one more day, and then we go to the Rethali palace, and you let us mourn."

Alex held his breath.

"What if we don't find her, but we find a lead?"

Weston sighed. "No. We don't have time for wild goose chases."

"Fine," Gareth grunted. "But I'm not happy."

"Do you think that I am?"

The whispered words hung in the air for a moment. Alex stared at his hideous claws, wondering again if he'd been wrong, and he should return Raelyn. Would King Weston listen to Alex's warning not to trust Henry? He barely managed not to snort aloud at the absurd idea of Weston even listening long enough for Alex to get a full sentence in.

"We fought a manticore," Gareth said, but much of the fight was gone from his voice. "Why is it so hard to believe some other beast took her? Those villagers claimed there's a dragon—"

Alex's heart nearly stopped.

"There's no dragon," Weston replied wearily. "You said yourself earlier today, there was no sign of a dragon where she was taken. The villagers weren't even sure it exists. And I'm not sure it would be any better if a dragon took her. They are harder to kill than a manticore."

"I'd kill it," Gareth insisted. "I'd rip out its heart with my bare hands if that's what it took to get Raelyn back."

Gooseflesh prickled Alex's arms, and he dug his claws into the dry dirt as he struggled to suppress his fear.

"I know you would, son."

Alex swallowed hard, scarcely daring to breathe.

"If—when we find her tomorrow…" The sound of a boot scuffing against the soil punctuated Gareth's hesitation. "You won't try to stop me from fighting whatever is holding her captive, will you? Person, monster, dragon, I don't care. It will die on my sword."

King Weston sighed. "I know I couldn't stop you, and even though I'd be afraid for you…if something is preventing her from returning to us, it would deserve a cruel death. Now come on. You'll want to rest before tomorrow."

Footsteps faded away back toward the camp.

Alex buried his face in his knees and cried silent tears—a skill he had mastered before he had his own room, when he didn't want to wake Meredith or the others. He needed to get out of there, far away from a camp full of knights who were probably on edge after a manticore attack and losing their princess. Far from a hurting, angry brother and father who had every reason to hate him. But he couldn't make his limbs move.

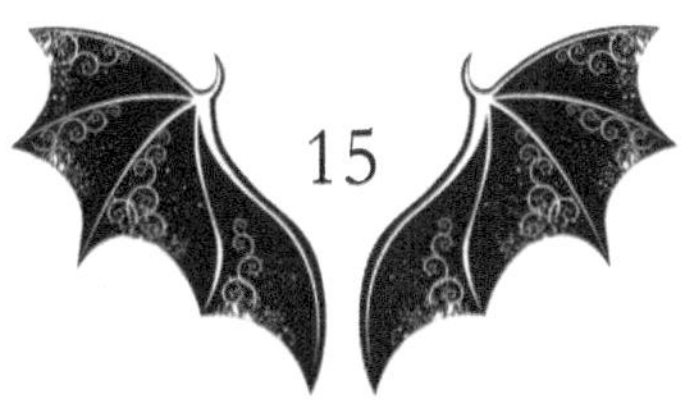

15

After everything that had happened the last two days, Alex felt drained. Gareth and Weston's conversation not only filled him with doubt, but dredged up memories of his parents, leaving his heart raw and bleeding. Like Weston, Alex's father had been a king first and father second, occasionally almost cold toward his son in his dedication to his kingdom and duty. But just like Weston loved his children, Alex's parents had loved him.

He was pretty sure they had, anyway. Sometimes he wasn't sure what parts of his memories of his parents were true, which were rose-tinted after years of missing them, and which were confused snippets of memories of his parents, nurses and tutors, and new adoptive family. At least Raelyn's family were all old enough they'd keep clear memories of her.

But she shouldn't be only a memory to them.

And yet, if she married Tristan, they would leave her alone in Rethalyon in the care of a murderer and curse-caster, and she might be only a memory, anyway.

Alex kept a frustrated growl behind his teeth as he finally stood. Silent as a cat, he wove through the forest until he was far enough from the Eynlaean camp to fly again.

It started to rain, and still he flew. His mind was a tumult of emotion and arguments, but when he focused on flying between the tips of pines, the chaos quieted. He lost track of how long he flew, but as lightning rent the sky overhead and the rain progressed from a steady sprinkle to a downpour, he forced himself to return to the cave. After pausing in the cave entrance to shake water off his wings and scaled tail, he headed to his room. Princess Raelyn had probably gone to bed hours ago, and even if she hadn't, he wasn't certain he could face her yet.

Water dripped from his soaked hair and clothes and the tips of his claws. He hoped it would dry by morning because he was too exhausted to clean it up. When he pushed open the door to his room, he was surprised to be greeted by a lively fire instead of the cold, dark room he expected.

The pinch in his brows smoothed as his gaze fell on his bed. Lucas lay sprawled over the mattress, one foot and one hand dangling off the edge, his hair messier than usual. Alex shook Lucas's shoulder.

"Keeping my bed warm for me?"

Lucas mumbled something incoherent and pushed Alex's arm away.

"Where am I supposed to sleep, oh keeper of the flame?"

Lucas opened one eye, looked at Alex for a moment, then rubbed his eyes. "Nightmare?"

"Only if we count you being in my bed as a nightmare."

"In your bed…" Lucas scrambled upright. "In your bed! I'm sorry, Alex! I meant to be waiting up for you." He blinked. "After Meredith told us you went out, Jasper was waiting up, but he was falling asleep in his chair, and that always makes his neck and back hurt, so I said I'd wait up in case you needed any help when you got home." Lucas tilted his head. "Or needed to talk."

Alex leaned one hand against the wall and started removing his boots with the other. "Thank you. I shouldn't have been out so late, I know."

Lucas watched him in silence, then asked quietly, "Did you really go to find Raelyn's family?"

Alex froze. "I...yes." He didn't look at Lucas as he placed his boots near the fire and sat down in front of the flames, spreading his cumbersomely large wings to help them dry and keep them from jabbing into the stone floor. "They didn't see me. I know how to be careful and silent. I just made sure they were alive. I can tell Princess Raelyn..."

He hung his head, unsure what he could tell her. That her family was alive but crushed by her disappearance? That they'd survived the manticore attack, but her presumed death was tearing them apart?

Lucas slid onto the floor next to him. "Are they not all right?"

"Yes...and no." Alex buried his face in his hands. "I don't know what to do. They're alive, but they're hurting. Her father is heartbroken and afraid of losing her brother, too. Her brother... He's convinced a monster"—his voice broke on the word—"has his sister. He's hurting and frightened and so, so angry. And I could fix it. I could give King Weston his daughter back so he wouldn't look so empty and wouldn't have to decide between letting his son look for her and his duty to his kingdom. I could give Prince Gareth his sister back." He winced. "Although I'm not sure that would be enough to quell his anger."

"Do you think he'd come after you?"

Alex dropped his hands and stared into the flames. "Prince Gareth is protective of his sister. Vehemently so. He said he'd rip out a dragon's heart with his bare hands to rescue her. If she told him I'd kept her here, that I turned into a dragon and threatened to eat her..." Human embarrassment heated his cheeks. "Yes. He might hunt me."

"We'd hide you," Lucas said. "We'd protect you."

"I know." Alex almost could have sobbed, but instead, he ruffled Lucas's hair. "But I don't think I could hide if any of you were potentially in danger." His momentary smile fell. "That's part of the problem. If I were in Gareth's place, and Raelyn was you…I might feel similarly."

"I can't imagine how I'd feel if you went missing." Lucas yawned. "Poor Prince Gareth. And Princess Raelyn."

"Yes." The scales of Alex's tail made a rasping sound against the stone as it curled and uncurled next to his crossed legs.

"So…you're taking her back, then?"

Alex groaned. "I've been debating that all night and am no closer to an answer."

"Well, what else—" Another yawn interrupted Lucas's words. "What else are you thinking? Jasper always says kings have to consider the arguments and decide which is stronger, right?"

"Really?" Alex bumped his shoulder into Lucas's. "Even without Jasper, I still get Jasper lectures?"

Lucas bumped him in return. "You just hate when I'm right. What are the arguments?"

With a sigh, Alex turned again toward the fire and leaned back on his hands. He was getting sleepy, but he needed to figure this out.

"If I keep Princess Raelyn here, her family will mourn her as dead. Their sorrow will be my fault."

Lucas rested his chin on his hand. "But isn't it also true she would have died if you hadn't saved her? Twice, between the wolves and the minotaur. So they would have mourned her, anyway. You didn't attack her caravan or spook her horse or get her lost. You saved her, even if they don't know that."

Alex stared at his brother. Lucas did kind of have a point, even if it was debatable.

"She'll miss them."

Lucas's eyes turned sad, but then he shrugged. "They were always going to leave her in Rethalyon."

Alex squinted, trying to determine when exactly Lucas had started acting so…grown up. "She might never truly forgive me. Might never like or trust me. And there might be tension as her father and Henry try to rework the treaty without her. Henry won't have any leverage against King Weston…I don't think. So they should work it out, but it will make things more difficult."

Lucas shifted so he could sit against the bed. "And if you take her back?"

"A lot of *mights*," Alex said heavily. "Princess Raelyn might tell Prince Gareth about me. He might try to kill me. Henry and Tristan might hear of me and try to find us. Well, me. We might have to move, might have to spend the rest of our lives afraid of being spotted or caught. It might put you all in harm's way unless we separated. Tristan might hurt Raelyn. He never even had a mother, and his father is a murderer, a usurper, a liar, and…well." He held out his arms to indicate himself.

Lucas nodded. "Curse-caster. Henry can't be trusted."

"Exactly. And not only would Raelyn be entering his court, becoming his daughter-in-law, she'd be married to *Tristan*. Who told me my mother deserved to die." A growl shook his chest, and he had to clear his throat and force himself to breathe. "I can't imagine they'd be kind to her. They might even threaten or hurt her to bully Eynlae. Or if the princess of Eynlae turned into a monster, that would probably break the treaty. I can't *know* they would do anything sinister…but sending her to them feels like sending a lamb into a lion's den. Well"—he considered—"a lamb with a bit of spark to her."

That won him a brief chuckle from Lucas. The crackling of the fire and sporadic drip from Alex's drying clothes punctuated the silence. Alex half expected Lucas to be asleep when he looked over again, but Lucas was staring intently into the distance.

"I don't want anything to happen to you," Lucas said at last. "And no matter what happens, we aren't separating. I might punch you if you ever suggested it, because family doesn't leave when it gets dangerous. But I think Raelyn has to stay. You're safer if you don't return her. So are Mom and Dad and Jasper, since Henry can't find out about them."

Alex cocked his head, nervous he'd said too much. "Why—"

"Dad told me." Lucas looked toward the fire. "They always told me to be discreet in the village, especially because I can talk so much and lose track of what I'm saying and might say something I shouldn't, so I have to be careful not to mention you, which is sad, but, anyway, a couple years ago, Dad decided I was old enough to understand why it was so important. So he told me they committed treason in hiding and helping you after Henry was crowned. You don't have to hide the truth from me, Alex. I know that if Henry caught us, we'd all die."

A lump caught in Alex's throat. "Come here." He patted the ground next to him. Lucas frowned, but Alex just patted it again. "Come on."

Lucas lifted a brow but did as he was told and moved closer again. As soon as he was near enough, Alex wrapped one wing around Lucas the way he had years ago, when they were younger, and Lucas was the one needing comfort after a normal childhood nightmare.

"I won't let that happen," Alex promised. "I won't put any of you in danger if I can avoid it. Including Raelyn."

"Maybe I could be a king," Lucas mused.

Alex blinked, fighting a laugh. "I'm sorry, what?"

"We seem to have agreed which argument was better." Lucas smirked up at him. "So that must mean I would do all right making rulings as a king. It doesn't seem *that* hard."

Alex knocked his wing against Lucas's shoulder. "Don't go getting any delusional ideas." He stood and offered his hand to Lucas. "We should both get to sleep."

Lucas took his hand, not even hesitating at Alex's claws. But then, Lucas couldn't remember Alex before he was cursed, so Lucas was even more comfortable with Alex's dragon features than Alex himself was.

"You need sleep more than I do," Lucas said as he stood.

"I look that tired?"

"No, you're going to want to be well-rested before the tongue-lashing Mom is going to give you tomorrow. Especially when she hears you approached the Eynlaean camp."

Alex grimaced. "I should have told Raelyn not to tell Meredith where I was going."

"Too late now. Need help getting that wet shirt off?"

"That'd be great, yes."

Once Lucas had helped him into a dry shirt, Lucas grabbed a torch from near the door and lit it. "Sleep well!"

"You too."

Lucas darted out, closing the door behind him, and Alex changed into dry trousers before slipping into bed. As Alex fell asleep, his last thought was wondering how he was going to face Raelyn the next morning.

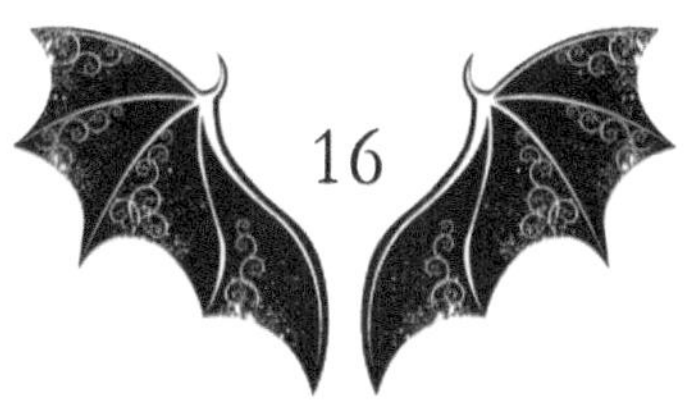

After so much shifting and flying and staying up late, Alex slept soundly until knocking on his door dragged him out of the blissful depths of slumber. "Come in," he called, his voice half muffled by his pillow.

Meredith entered, a candle in hand, and a hard look on her face that had Alex wishing he hadn't admitted her. The low flames from the fireplace reflected in her eyes, as if offering a warning about the fire about to erupt.

"Of all the stupid—"

"Mer, please, don't." Alex sat up with a groan and stretched, working out a crick in his neck. As he stood, he shook out his wings and tail before dragging his gaze back to Meredith's pinched expression. "I was careful."

"You could have been killed!" Meredith jabbed his chest with the forefinger of her free hand. "You could have been seen! What do you think the king of Eynlae would do if he saw you? Did you think that wouldn't come up when he speaks with Henry? Did you think they wouldn't get curious and even suspicious and try to find you?"

Alex rubbed his forehead. "Meredith—"

"Do you have any idea how worried we all were?"

"I didn't mean for you to worry," he murmured. "I hadn't meant for you to know—"

"Oh, excellent, so if they *had* killed or captured you, we wouldn't have even known what happened." She poked his chest again, harder, and the dragon grew restless. "Do you know the horrible thoughts of what they might do to you that tormented me all night? The ways they might torture you—"

"You know I'd escape. I can breathe fire and shift now." Alex smiled, ignoring the similar fears he'd had, but Meredith just scowled. He dropped the smile with a sigh. "I'm sorry. But I *was* careful. They didn't see me, and I needed to do this for her. Raelyn is alone. You were worried last night, but that's how worried she's been about her family since she woke up here. She deserves to know that her family is all right."

Meredith opened her mouth, closed it, and her hard expression eased as her shoulders slumped. She tapped his chest again, much softer this time. "You have a good heart in there, Alexander."

"Thanks to you." Alex patted her arm, then gave her a mischievous smile and winked. "Although you've been so hard on Raelyn, I'm beginning to wonder if I learned kindness from you, after all."

She wrinkled her nose. "You need to stop growing up. You and Lucas both. I keep forgetting he's fifteen, and then he says something that sounds all grown up or I realize again how tall he's getting, and…I'm not ready to let either of you go."

"Don't worry." Alex pressed a kiss to her auburn hair. "You're stuck with me forever."

Meredith pulled back from him and frowned. "Don't talk like that."

His heart sank. Every time he cracked a joke about or mentioned his suspicion that he'd be cursed for the rest of his life, the others reacted with shock, disappointment, anger, scolding, or a mixture of all of them. Keeping up the charade that someday he'd be human and reclaim his throne was growing tiring. But he couldn't argue with Meredith, especially when she had barely forgiven him for his stunt the previous night, so he turned away.

"I'm going to tell Princess Raelyn what I learned." He gulped as he sat on his bed and pulled on his boots.

For a moment, Meredith stood watching him. "Do you need support?"

Alex stood and shook his head. "No. I should do this alone."

She appeared unconvinced but nodded. "I'll be in the kitchen finishing breakfast."

"Thank you."

Alex hurried to Lucas's—now Raelyn's—room, worried that she'd be up and looking for breakfast before he got there. But when he reached the room, he stopped outside the closed door, his skin going clammy. The dragon stirred at his nervousness, and he closed his eyes and took a moment to breathe. How much would she want to know? How much did he dare tell her? Would she accept that they were alive and mostly unharmed and be all right with that?

He raised his fist to knock and hesitated. Since he could see fine without light, he hadn't brought a candle or torch, but Raelyn wouldn't be able to see him. Maybe he should go get one first... *You're stalling.* With one last fortifying inhale, he forced himself to knock.

The door opened almost immediately, the bright flare of a candle illuminating the hope burning in Raelyn's beautiful eyes. Alex's mouth went dry.

Just say something! "Your brother sustained a minor injury, but your family is alive."

The princess sagged against the side of the open door, and a slight upward curve pulled at her lips. "You saw them? Where? Are they still on the pass?"

He looked at the ground, unable to bear that hopeful expression any longer. Those were the exact questions he was afraid to answer because he'd have to decide how truthful he was going to be. But in that moment, he realized if he wanted Princess Raelyn to ever trust him, he needed to be honest with her—even though it meant she might not like him. She deserved that. Still, it took a moment for him to force the words out, and he couldn't look at her as he admitted, "They're still in the mountains. Looking for you."

Raelyn backed away, distancing herself from him. He raised his gaze from the ground to her pale face and guessed the questions behind her darting eyes.

"They aren't close," he said softly. "And there's no trail for them to follow. I flew you here."

She put more space between them, her shoulders rising and falling with every breath. "How do you know my brother is hurt?"

Alex shifted, the memory of Gareth's fury like a brand in his mind. "Because I saw him having a heated argument with your father about whether to keep looking for you."

As she placed the candle on the little table and braced herself against it, he wished he could go to her and comfort her. Maybe he should have had Meredith accompany him, because there was nothing he could do but tell Raelyn things that would hurt her.

"Who won?" Raelyn whispered.

His wings twitched as the urge to flee the conversation grew. "Your father agreed to search for one more day. Then they will go to the Rethali palace to break the news that…you're dead."

Her strangled sob chipped at his heart. She turned her face away from him as a tremor went through her, and Alex mentally kicked himself. What did he do now? Was there anything he could do to give her any comfort when she doubtless blamed him? She probably didn't want to be anywhere near him.

He hazarded a question of his own. "Do you want your breakfast in your room?"

"I'm not hungry," she snapped without looking at him.

Alex stood in the doorway, searching for words that wouldn't come. There were no words for this. "I'm sorry," he said finally. He closed the door and leaned his forehead against the wood, listening closely.

After a moment, a puff of breath and the faint scent of smoke indicated she'd blown out her candle. Shuffling footsteps and a quiet creak were followed by silence. She'd gone back to bed. Alex sighed and left her alone.

The guilt and nagging feeling he needed to *do* something to fix this gnawed at him all morning—while he ate breakfast and barely listened to Jasper and Peter taking their turn expressing their disappointment with his life choices, while he practiced swordplay with Lucas and Peter, and while he freshened up afterward.

When he entered the dining room for dinner, Jasper looked over at him from where he was already seated at the table. "Meredith and I were just discussing if someone should check in on Princess Raelyn."

Alex stiffened. He wasn't sure he could face her again. But more importantly… "I don't think she wants to see me." He slid into his chair and slouched down. "Her family is looking for her, even though her parents think she's dead, but they're only looking for one more day. She didn't take that well."

"You told her all of that?" Jasper asked with evident surprise.

Alex shrugged, glancing over at Meredith and Lucas as they pushed the rattling cart of food toward the table from the kitchen. "She deserved the truth. I won't win her friendship on false terms. I've done enough damage already." He held his head in his hands and groaned. "But she hates me now, and I have no idea how to fix it. I'm not sure I can."

"Why does her opinion matter so much?" Meredith asked.

Alex tossed his hands up and leaned back in his chair. "Because she's living here, and it'll be perfectly miserable if she hates me? Because I want another friend? Because Henry and Tristan are more than enough enemies for me? Because I want her to like me?"

"Because she's pretty?" Lucas asked with a waggle of his eyebrows as he helped Meredith set the table.

Heat spread over Alex's face, so he did the mature thing and stuck his tongue out at Lucas, just as Peter entered the room from the far end, opposite from Alex's room.

"I see all attempts at etiquette lessons are still failing," Peter said as he strolled over to the table. He kissed Meredith's cheek before sitting down.

"Who is going to judge me?" Alex demanded. "The stalactites?"

Jasper raised his brows.

"Oh, hush." Alex frowned as Lucas placed a plate in front of Raelyn's chair at the far end of the table. "Wait. Perhaps someone—not me—could take Raelyn her food in her room after we eat?"

Everyone stared at him, making him self-conscious. "She needs to eat, but…I doubt she wants to be around me right now."

Meredith nodded and took the plate back from Lucas, loading it with a slice of the meat pie and covering it before she took her own seat. Alex cut himself a piece while everyone else did likewise.

"Now," Jasper said, "about your manners, Alex."

"Jasper," Alex groaned. "We have a rule! No lectures during meals!"

"A very good rule," Lucas said around a mouthful of food.

Peter sighed heavily and Meredith looked heavenward.

Jasper motioned toward Lucas. "Ah, but what if the lecture is *about* meals? Both of you have so little decorum, and neither of you are children anymore. Lucas is a year away from being of marriageable age—"

Lucas choked on his food, then took a large gulp of water. "I'm all right." Alex had to fight a laugh, and he was glad he had when he saw Meredith's strained expression.

"Just because young people *do* get married at sixteen hardly means they should," Meredith protested, spinning her fork between her fingers.

"Alex, however," Peter interrupted, "is certainly old enough to know better than to make faces at the dinner table."

Alex barely stopped himself from rolling his eyes. "It's only us and Lucas."

"And now a princess," Jasper reminded him.

"Oh, fine, but we *do* live in a cave. I rather doubt she has very high expectations about our manners—" He stopped, his mind emptying and tongue sticking to the roof of his mouth as his gaze caught on a figure on the other side of the room. Raelyn walked toward the table, her steps small and her shoulders hunched.

She'd come on her own. And she was looking at him. Was she here to yell at him? What should he say? His entire body seemed to have frozen as the princess drew closer.

"Lucas?" Raelyn asked, and Alex fought some disappointment that she hadn't addressed him. "I'm sorry. I shouldn't have yelled at you. Actually...I should have listened to you."

Lucas had turned toward her, and he seemed to consider his response. A new panic rose in Alex's mind. What if his *family* couldn't forgive her?

"I forgive you," Lucas said brightly, and Alex relaxed a little. "At least you don't make me smell like smoke when you lose your temper and shout at me." He cast a sly glance at Alex, who fought the urge to stick his tongue out again.

"Um. Thank you." Raelyn looked at the empty chair but didn't move to take it.

Alex stood, abruptly remembering himself. "I was going to have Meredith bring you dinner…after…" He gulped, wondering now if it'd been rude to not have her food brought sooner. "I didn't want to bother…" *He* was the problem here. "Do you want me to go?"

Raelyn blinked. "This is your home; I can't kick you out."

He mussed his hair, wishing the twitchy feeling in his tail would abate. "It's your home now, too."

A shadow passed over her face, and Alex had the impression he'd said the wrong thing. He cleared his throat and looked to Meredith. "Where's her food?"

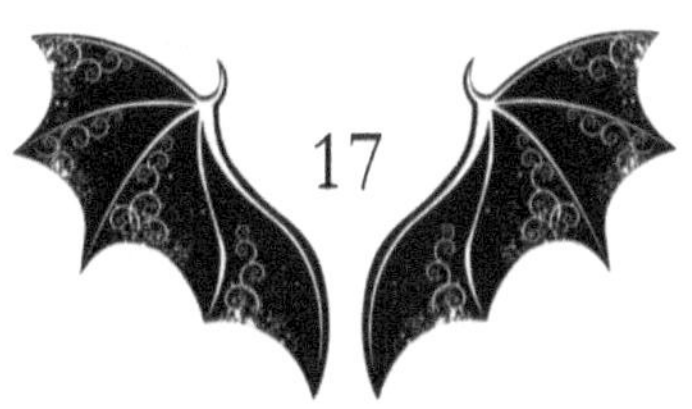

17

Meredith hurried to the cart and uncovered Raelyn's food.

"You can take it to your room, if you would prefer," Alex said, hating how his voice rasped. "You're free to stay, too." He hoped that hadn't sounded too desperate.

Raelyn took her seat at the end of the table. "I think I'll eat here. Thank you."

Alex finally let himself truly breathe as he sat back down. "Good. Good."

As Meredith gave Raelyn her food and the princess started eating, Alex dared to entertain the possibility that friendship wasn't hopeless. And if that wasn't hopeless, maybe even more was possible, too...

"How are you feeling?" Meredith patted Raelyn's arm in passing, and Raelyn jerked away with a pained gasp, snapping Alex back to the present. Meredith clenched her hand over her chest with a horrified expression. "I'm sorry! I forgot."

"Forgot what?" Alex demanded, moving his attention from Meredith to the princess. "Are you hurt?"

Raelyn hunched over the table. "Just bruises."

"Bruises?" He hadn't realized she was hurt badly enough for a mere touch to cause her pain. "Show me."

"It's nothing," Raelyn started, but Alex didn't believe that for a moment. He shoved out of his chair, worry and some re-emerging anger at the minotaur and himself making his movements stiff.

"Show me," he repeated as he approached the princess.

Raelyn looked away as she pushed her sleeve up past a huge yellow discoloration with darker blue-black bruises in the shape of a minotaur hand. Dragon rage flared as she dropped the sleeve, and he had to work hard to keep his voice even and quiet.

"Both arms?"

Raelyn nodded.

He knelt beside her chair. "Princess." He waited until she met his eyes. "If you ask me to, I will hunt the minotaur down and burn it alive." His family all began talking at once, probably trying to remind him that he had a no killing code for a reason, but he held up his hand to silence them.

"Why?" Raelyn asked.

"Because it hurt you." Alex's tail thrashed as he worked to keep his emotions under control. "Because I want you to believe that I don't want you hurt. I know you don't want to stay here, and I know killing it won't make it up to you, but maybe…maybe it's something." Maybe this could be the thing he'd felt like he needed to do all morning, the way that he proved to her that he cared and wanted to protect her—not just from minotaurs, but from Henry and Tristan, too.

But she shook her head. "It won't change or fix anything."

His hope he'd found an answer to his feeling of uselessness evaporated. "All right." He dragged himself back to his seat at the head of the table and forced himself to continue eating in the awkward silence.

Did Raelyn understand his reasoning? Or did she just think the offer to hunt down the minotaur reinforced his monstrous side? Jasper and the others were doubtless judging him for even considering breaking his commitment to non-violence for a girl.

Alex cut the side of his fork through a bit of flaky pastry crust, avoiding looking at anyone around the table. Lucas's voice broke the uncomfortable quiet.

"So…you saw Alex naked?"

Across the table, Raelyn choked, and Alex would've been coughing, too, if he'd been eating or drinking at that moment. He stared at his meat pie like he had spotted a bit of gold hidden in the gravy as he fought the urge to smirk at Raelyn, recalling her abrupt declaration that she'd noticed his state of undress.

"Lucas!" Meredith gasped, and it was all Alex could do to keep from laughing even as his face heated.

"What on earth, Lucas?" By the sound of Peter's tone, he was not impressed with his son's question.

"I just was wondering if she, that is…" Lucas faltered. "What she thought."

Alex slyly looked across the table, noticing Lucas's hunched posture and Raelyn's scarlet face. He was annoyed when Jasper spoke up, saving Raelyn from having to answer.

"Why, Lucas?" Oh, Alex recognized that tone. Jasper's sensibilities had been properly shocked. That lecture about proper manners was going to be *so* much worse now. "What exactly are you thinking?"

Lucas was blushing. "Alex looks… I dunno, based on what the girls in the village say about the village boys, girls would probably think he's attractive. But if Princess Raelyn doesn't think Alex is attractive…"

Alex held his breath. Could she have changed her mind about whether he was repulsive or handsome? Did he even want to know? This was a disaster; he should say something. The problem was, he hadn't the faintest idea what to say to make this any less embarrassing—or to cover his secret hope that Raelyn did approve of his muscled chest.

Then, to his utter confusion, Raelyn laughed. She covered her mouth, as if trying to stifle her amusement, but then her shoulders started to shake. Alex raised his head, staring at her now. She laughed until her eyes watered, and Alex found himself fighting laughter, especially when he noticed Jasper staring at the princess with a deep furrow between his brows. The old steward had probably hoped a princess would bring some decorum to the cave, but Alex was getting the impression this was *not* the princess to choose for such a task.

Raelyn finally got her laughter under control. "Oh, Lucas. You're handsome. Don't let the village girls make you doubt it."

Alex's smile dropped as his amusement faded away.

"I'm actually available for the first time in my life," Raelyn added with a contemplative look at Lucas. "How old are you, anyway?"

Alex eyed Lucas. He'd realized his brother was growing up…he hadn't considered exactly what that meant. A year sounded like a long time when Jasper mentioned it offhandedly, but now it suddenly seemed much shorter. If Alex recalled the details of the treaty and had done his math correctly, Raelyn was eighteen, which meant there were as many years between him and Raelyn as there were between Raelyn and Lucas. He'd thought the ultimate torture would be if Raelyn stayed and always found him hideous while he fell for her, but if Raelyn stayed and Alex fell for her while she eventually fell in love with Lucas, that might break him.

"F-f-fifteen." Lucas gulped, and Alex took some satisfaction from how unprepared Lucas was for Raelyn's attention.

"Barely," Jasper scoffed, helping to calm Alex's tension. Next to Alex, Meredith was attempting to hide her snickers behind her hand, and Peter looked like he was struggling not to laugh. At least none of them seemed to think Lucas a serious contender for Raelyn's affections…unless Alex was misinterpreting their reactions.

"My birthday was a month ago." Lucas slouched further in his chair.

"Well, you've been fifteen longer than I've been eighteen," Raelyn said with a laugh.

Alex frowned at his dinner. It shouldn't bother him. There was no reason to care. Raelyn was never his, and he'd known she wouldn't fall for him. He didn't love her, anyway. He'd known her for two days, and she'd yelled at him several times in that span. Ridiculous. He didn't even like her…that much.

Raelyn leaned back in her chair. "Thank you, Lucas. I needed that."

Alex eyed her as she went back to eating, trying to decide if Raelyn had been teasing Lucas or what under the stars had just happened.

"Um…you're welcome?" Lucas rolled his eyes and smiled, sending a confused glance and a shrug toward Alex. Alex shrugged in response.

After Meredith and Lucas cleared the table and Jasper and Peter headed out together, Alex and Raelyn were left alone at the table. As if noticing Alex's stare, Raelyn fidgeted with her braid. The question of whether she had any genuine interest in Lucas gnawed at him.

"Lucas is…attractive?" He tried to keep his tone light and uninvested, but wasn't sure he succeeded.

A bit of pink tinged Raelyn's cheeks as she shrugged. "For a fifteen-year-old. I don't know. I never really bothered to think about if men were handsome, since it didn't matter."

Despite himself, amusement crept back in. With the way she avoided looking at his naked chest and was blushing right now? "I rather doubt that," he said.

"I'm not talking to you about this." Her little huff as she crossed her arms only confirmed Alex's suspicion, but he decided not to keep teasing her.

"All right, Princess." He tapped his claws on the tabletop, trying to determine how to fill the silence. He thought again of her bruises with a flare of emotion. "I do feel badly about…everything. Keeping you here. The minotaur. Your family. I wish there was a way…" He couldn't bear looking at her any longer, so he shifted his attention to the fire. "I just can't."

After a moment, Raelyn murmured, "I understand."

"You do?" Alex stared at her, certain he must have misheard.

"I don't like it." She placed her elbows on the table, her hands resting on the sides of her neck. "But I understand. Maybe Henry's changed. But if he hasn't, if he's so heartless… I don't know if I want to marry Prince Tristan."

Alex's lungs shuddered, and his tail went completely still, as if it, too, were listening.

"I hate that I can't know if they would use me against my father or not," Raelyn continued. "But… Meredith told me Henry cursed you. If that's true, I can't blame you for fearing and hating him enough to want to keep me here. But…I still don't like it."

Alex glanced down at his clawed hands. "I suppose that's fair." It was progress, he told himself. At least she understood and was starting to believe him, even if she still didn't like him. Well, he had better things to occupy his time than sitting around with a princess who didn't want him there. He stood and headed for the exit to the mountain.

"Wait." The princess practically tripped out of her chair as she hurried…to follow him? Alex stopped as she asked, "Where are you going?"

He tilted his head, his eyebrows pinching. Was she about to yell at him again? "Why?"

"I…" Raelyn crossed an arm over her stomach, holding her other arm against her side. Still shielding herself from him, consciously or not. "I don't want to sit in my room all afternoon. And I don't know where the others went… I'd like to go outside."

He should have realized. Of course she wouldn't want to stay couped up in the dark any more than he did. "I'm going out to check some of the bigger traps. Care to join me?" he added, half expecting she wouldn't be interested in spending that much time with him.

Instead, she smiled at him—at *him*—and said, "Yes, please."

18

The princess trailed Alexander through the forest. She was distracting.

Not in the way Lucas was. She only made a couple of attempts at conversation, whereas Lucas filled the air with his talking. Despite her relative silence, she was infinitely more distracting, because where Lucas was comfortable and his exuberance familiar, Raelyn was...

Well, to start, suspicious.

The moment they walked out of the cave, it occurred to Alex that this entire thing might be a charade. For all he knew, she was so calm because she'd grabbed another knife and was planning to stab him in the back. He glanced at her, relaxing when he confirmed her hands were empty and there didn't appear to be anywhere in her simple dress where she could have stashed a knife. But they'd be entering the forest, and Raelyn might have it in her head to sneak off. Recalling the bruises on her arms, he dismissed that thought. Surely she wouldn't be so foolish as to try that again...right?

As she continued to follow him and sat down and waited patiently every time he stopped to inspect or reset a trap, he decided it wasn't a ruse, and she wasn't going to attempt to attack him or run away.

Well, Princess Raelyn might not be plotting anything, but she was still a pretty young woman, and the desire to stare at her was overwhelming.

She'd washed her face and redone the braid in her golden hair. Her shining blue eyes took in everything in the forest, and whenever she saw something that caught her fancy, her soft pink lips curved into a gentle smile that did strange things to Alex's heart. But even when she was behind him, he was acutely aware of her presence—and of the fact that she was walking with him peaceably, without mockery. Her hands swung gently at her sides and her stance was more relaxed than he'd ever seen, although she kept some distance between them and occasionally cast him a nervous glance.

If only he could find a way to connect with her and prove that she needn't fear him. So far, conversation hadn't proved very effective. But one thing had… An idea occurred to him, and he grinned. He rushed through checking the final trap and headed away from the cave. This was brilliant. A way for them to have fun together, for him to show her a side of himself that wasn't dangerous. Maybe she'd even want to participate, and he could hold her in his arms again—

"Any more traps?" Raelyn's voice startled him out of his thoughts.

"No."

"Are we going back, then?"

Had she tired of being around him? "No."

After a moment, Raelyn spoke again, a bit of nervousness seeping into her tone. "Then where are we going?"

There wasn't a good way to explain their destination or what he had planned without spoiling the surprise, and they were almost there, so he just said, "You'll see."

Sure enough, he reached the cliff a few minutes later, and he motioned to the princess to join him on the edge. "Ah. Here we are."

"Oh…" Raelyn's mouth fell open as she took in the scene before them.

It was one of Alex's favorite views. The cliff overlooked a lake that was surrounded by mountains covered in jagged lines of granite between forests of pine. In the late afternoon sun, the view shone in shades of turquoise and emerald, with distant snowcapped peaks glittering like diamonds. With a satisfied glance at the rapturous look on Raelyn's face, Alex perched on the edge of the cliff, letting his legs dangle.

"It's beautiful," Raelyn said softly.

Alexander looked out over the landscape, a grin pulling at his mouth, and patted the stony cliff. "Come on, Princess."

"That…seems unsafe."

He chuckled. "Only if you jump or something crazy. But don't worry. If you fall, I'll catch you." Was this flirting? It felt like flirting. If it was, he was enjoying it immensely.

"I don't know—"

"Aw, fine. Be boring." He stood and let his smile grow as he backed toward the edge. Jasper always teased Alex about his "flair for the dramatic," but Alex had never wanted to show off to someone so badly in his life. "I, on the other hand, like to live life on the edge." With that, he stepped off the precipice, more than a little smug when he heard the princess gasp before the rush of wind filled his ears.

He opened his wings with a snap and flew upward, his spirit soaring, especially when he saw that Raelyn had run nearly to the edge, her face white with panic. She cared—about *him*.

Oh, he was definitely going to show off. He cartwheeled backward, flapped his wings until he caught a draft, then soared over the lake, his tail helping him move the direction he wanted to go with scarcely a thought. The wind created by his speed rustled his hair around his ears and horns. He closed his eyes, lost for a moment in the freedom of flight as he tucked his wings and tail and rolled sideways, bringing the motion to a stop by spreading his wings again.

With his wings extended, he felt powerful and untouchable, and even his sorrows, fears, hurts, and the weight of the curse fell away. As he hovered, he looked toward Raelyn. No fear reflected in her expression, just amazement as one of her soft smiles graced him.

Watch this, Princess. He folded his wings and dove sideways, plummeting toward the lake as his heart pounded, his pulse loud in his ears. As he felt an upward draft, he opened his wings and drifted up before flying down so close to the lake he could have reached down and touched the water. As much fun as he was having, he still probably shouldn't leave Princess Raelyn alone for *too* long. His tail curved as he turned and then flew high above her before coming to land on the cliff.

He leaned forward, catching his breath. "What. A. Rush!"

Raelyn lifted a brow. "Show-off."

Alex straightened and scratched the back of his head, unable to suppress his grin or the giddy twitch of his tail, but he decided to feign innocence. "What? Not at all. Unless I need to tell the eagle he's a show-off next time I see him diving at fish in the lake." He winked and could have sworn that she blushed. Flirting might be his new favorite hobby. He was about to offer to fly her over the lake when he realized how low the sun was getting. Evening fell quickly in the mountains as the peaks blocked the sunlight, and they didn't have torches, so it would be best if they returned before it got dark.

"We should head back." He probably shouldn't press his luck with the princess, anyway. She was finally looking at him like he might truly be more than a monster, and he didn't want to jeopardize that. They would just peacefully walk home.

As with everything with his troublesome princess, though, things didn't go to plan. Not when she got him to swear to answer some questions truthfully, and then asked if his mother had been a sorceress.

The question had caught him by surprise, stirring up his emotions and the dragon with them. "That's what you were told?" Alex asked as smoke escaped from his nostrils and his vision took on a crimson hue. "My uncle spread that lie—about his own sister—all the way to Eynlae?"

In response, Raelyn only nodded, her chin trembling.

No—he was scaring her again. He forced his breaths to slow and closed his eyes for a moment, focusing on cooling his anger and soothing his hurt. "Sorry." He opened his eyes and was relieved to see the world returned to its normal colors. "Did you have more questions?"

Raelyn hesitated, fiddling with the skirt of her dress. "What happened to your father?"

Short, dark hair and intimidating, mossy green eyes above a gentle smile flashed through Alex's mind. "He loved my mother. Her death nearly broke him. And then…he started acting peculiar. Hallucinating. Sleep walking. My uncle spread rumors. Jasper thinks my uncle poisoned both my parents." He took a deep breath, willing himself to stay calm while he remembered the shock of Jasper telling him that his father was dead. "One day, my father went for a walk and didn't come back. His body was mangled by crows when they found it, but he'd been stabbed through the heart. My uncle covered that up."

"And…then he cursed you," Raelyn supplied.

Alex nodded, hoping she didn't want him to explain. "I can't talk about…it. I physically can't."

"Is there anything you can tell me?" She said it so softly, like she was genuinely trying to understand, that Alex had to try. He might not get another chance to convince her.

"After…" Heavens above, this was harder than he'd imagined it'd be, especially when the dragon became restless as he poked at a wound he usually kept covered. "After my father's death, the Court of Lords decided to make me king under a regent until I turned eighteen. My uncle said he should be regent. The Lords must have doubted his motives because they appointed another lord instead. Someone who could have no legitimate claim to the throne. Shortly after that, my uncle disappeared for a week. He showed up just before my coronation, claiming he had talked to someone who knew my mother had used dark magic on me. More likely, he was hunting down some witch or sorcerer or fae for the—" His vocal cords seized. In his panic and frustration, he snorted more smoke. "I woke up in the middle of the night—"

The curse wouldn't let him say a word about his transformation or his uncle's presence, instead clamping over his throat like an invisible vice.

Alex ground his teeth, trying to figure out what he could say that would also help Raelyn understand how despicable Henry was. "The next day…" He stared at the ground, the memory still fresh even twelve years later, like an injury that sent shooting pain through his entire body if touched. "Henry dragged me, horns, wings, tail and all, before the Court of Lords and ranted about my parents' wickedness, and…and…"

'Here's your future king. I warned you, but you wouldn't listen. Look at this disfigured spawn of sorcery." Alex could practically feel the ropes chafing his wrists, the strain on his skull as Henry pulled him by a horn, the pain radiating up into his spine as a boot crushed his tail.

Trembling moved through his body, and he turned away from Raelyn before she could see the tears in his eyes. His wings shuddered as he resisted the urge to flee, even though the danger wasn't present. *Breathe, Alexander, breathe.* If Princess Raelyn were ever going to understand why he couldn't let her marry Tristan, she needed to know how Henry had accused him and his mother of being evil while Alex couldn't defend himself because the curse tightened around his vocal cords, cutting off his air. The memory was too raw, and he couldn't stop the tears that slipped out of his eyes.

Tell her.

"He said…" The emotional pain overwhelmed him, agitating the dragon, and Alexander released a roar as he directed his frantic energy into clawing at a nearby aspen. He was probably scaring the princess, but he could hardly think past the dragon heat spreading through his midsection and the sobs trapped in his lungs. With another roar to drown out the dragon's desire for vengeance, Alex fell to his knees and squeezed the sides of his head.

I am human. I am not anything Henry made me out to be. He took a purposeful breath and let it out slowly while he thought of Jasper, Meredith, Peter, Lucas, and even the girl standing behind him, her breaths quick and panicked, but despite his outburst…she wasn't running. His racing heartbeat calmed. The princess wasn't running.

She believed him. And she was trusting him enough to stay as he fought the dragon.

He opened his eyes, willing the dragon to quiet. The scarlet light receded from his vision, and he knew he would be all right.

"I'm sorry," he said quietly, not entirely sure if he was apologizing for not being able to explain or for his brief lapse of control. "I relive that day enough in my nightmares." He drew a steadying breath and skipped ahead in his story. "I managed to get away and hide. Thankfully, Jasper found me before my uncle did. He and the others helped me escape and have been with me ever since. That's the truth. As much of it as I can tell you. I swear it."

"I'm sorry," Raelyn whispered.

"Yes, well." Alex stood and turned around to face her again, desperately trying to determine some way to lighten the mood. "I can fly." He tried to smile, but it felt more like a grimace. "Is that all, Princess?"

"Have you told me everything about why you're keeping me here?"

"Yes," he replied, but he immediately realized that wasn't entirely true. At least, not anymore. "Mostly."

"Wh…what?"

Oh, why had he promised her complete honesty?

"Yes, I think it would be unjust for you to marry Tristan while I hide in a cave and Henry sits on my father's throne," Alex said, staring at a small green bud trying to push up through dead foliage from last fall. "Yes, I believe you'd be in danger in Henry's court, and I'm afraid of Henry finding out about me and my family. But since I promised the complete truth…" He looked up, right into her earnest sapphire eyes, and his cheeks heated. He lowered his gaze again. "I'm jealous. It's harder when—when I think you're beautiful."

A snapping twig drew his attention back to Raelyn. She'd gone white as snow.

"I don't want you to think I want to…to marry you or anything," he said hastily. Oh, no, that might lead her to conclude that he wasn't interested. "Not that I actively don't want that, I'm not averse or something—I…" He groaned, cursing his flustered mind. "You're so…small and gentle. When you're not angry or afraid, you have a sweet side. The side that cares about your family, that listens and apologizes. And even when you were terrified, you were clever enough to try to reason and bargain with me. And when you laugh…" He smiled, but stopped himself before he could say anything too embarrassing. "You're too good for my cousin and uncle. Maybe Henry has changed, or I'm wrong about him. But in his story, in his world, I'm the villain." He lowered his head, his heart sinking down to his boots. "I can't stand the thought of you believing him."

"I wouldn't believe him."

He desperately wished that were true. "You did before. Eventually, you'd only remember the dragon. The horned creature with red eyes who…" He shook his head, the idea too painful to continue. "I keep hoping I can convince you I'm not a monster. I feel like I need to, even though I don't know exactly why it's so important."

And yet, despite all his intentions, he kept frightening her. With a heavy sigh, he turned back toward the cave. "It's getting late. Meredith will be irritated if we're late for supper."

Teasing had always been one of Alex's preferred ways to show affection, particularly to Lucas, but he was quickly discovering teasing a pretty girl had a *very* different feeling. The line between friendly teasing and outright flirting was very thin, but he didn't even care to try to stop himself from crossing it. Especially since when Princess Raelyn got flustered, she also became more relaxed and fun. He much preferred gently teasing her about her unexpected and baffling love for goats or her height over actual arguments or her probing questions about his curse and his past. And when she teased him back, complaining about his long "stupid legs," he felt like doing a flying somersault.

The princess was more friendly at supper, too…at least, until she mentioned her family, and then she grew quiet, her smiles and laughter coming slower. Alex hated it. It probably shouldn't have bothered him so much, nor should he have felt the need to do something about it. She wasn't being antagonistic or defensive anymore, at least, and what did Alex owe her? *She* was the one who had gotten herself lost and attacked by wolves and minotaurs and made his life more complicated and dangerous and interesting—no, not interesting, annoying. All right, maybe more interesting, too.

As Alex helped clear the table of dishes after supper, he noted Raelyn looking increasingly more distraught. She worried her lower lip, her brows pinched, and her knuckles were nearly white as she gripped the arms of her chair.

He turned from the cart. "Are you all right, Princess?"

"Yes." The word came out too quickly, and she immediately winced. "No."

As if sensing a potentially awkward discussion incoming, Meredith shooed the others out, pushing the cart so quickly toward the kitchen the dishes threatened to rattle right off. In a moment of panic, Alex almost asked one of them to stay. He wasn't sure his heart could handle another difficult conversation so soon after the last one.

Instead, he let them go, pulled out Peter's chair next to hers, and sat down, a rush of relief going through him when Raelyn didn't move away or seem perturbed by his nearness. The seconds trickled by as he waited in silence, unwilling to push her and upset their delicate relationship.

"This morning," she said without looking at him, "you said you would kill the minotaur if I asked."

Oh. What had sounded like a good idea that morning no longer seemed wise—or pleasant. But if that's what she needed to trust him, he would do it. "Yes."

"I don't need that," she said, and he nearly slumped with relief. "But…" She lifted her gaze to his eyes. "There is something else."

Alex leaned on the table. "Something else…that could help make things up to you?" He held his breath as she nodded.

"Something that would make this—staying here—easier."

He sat up straighter, and his wings and tail twitched with excitement. "I'll do it if I can."

"You can say no. I'm not trying to trick you."

That was concerning, and like a bucket of cold water thrown on his head. "All right…"

"I…" The princess's cheeks pinked, and she glanced around. "I want to see my family."

Alex frowned. Meredith would kill him.

"From a distance," Raelyn hurried to add. "They don't need to see me. I wouldn't try to get their attention, I promise. You…" She swallowed hard. "You can gag me, if…if that would help. I'd just like to see them. One last time."

He absolutely wouldn't be gagging her, but could he trust her? Even if she kept her promise, going so close would be dangerous—even more so than when he'd gone by himself. Because if Gareth saw Alex with Raelyn, Alex didn't doubt the prince would kill him. He looked away from Raelyn's desperate eyes. "I don't know…"

"Please. Please."

What if seeing them only made her detest him more? Even if they weren't caught, this could undo all the progress they had made. But if he refused, that might make her hate him, anyway. He reluctantly met her eyes.

"Would this help you believe I'm not a monster?"

"I already believe that, or I wouldn't ask."

That didn't feel like one of her lies. Maybe he was being foolish, but he believed her.

"It will help me say goodbye," Raelyn continued before he could reply. "I need that closure. Just to see them, with my own eyes."

Alex's heart ached for the emotion in her voice, and he realized he would always regret not giving her this chance.

"I promise, I won't shout or try to run away or anything, but you can—"

"All right," he said.

Raelyn's broad smile wavered. "…really?"

"Do you want to go now?" he asked, afraid if they delayed, either his fear would win out or one of the others would discover their plan and put a stop to it.

"I would like that. If you're sure."

"If that's what you want." He stood and led the way out. "Let's go."

This was a terrible idea. Meredith and Jasper might actually lock him in his room after this, assuming he even made it back. *Stop it.* He couldn't think like that. They would be careful, and Raelyn would keep her word as a princess. Assuming she even believed that promises to monsters were worth keeping. No, he reminded himself. She said she believed he wasn't a monster, and he was choosing to trust her—just like she was trusting him.

As they walked out under the stars, Alex realized he hadn't fully thought this through. Why did this ridiculous princess keep addling his mind? They'd have to fly to reach her family…which provided an excellent opportunity to tease and flirt with the princess. He buried his fears under an air of levity and faced her. "There are three ways we can do this."

"See my family?"

"Get to them, anyway." Alex held up one finger. "One, we walk. That's not actually an option if you want to get there. Especially on your legs." He barely managed to keep his expression blank when she frowned in annoyance. He uncurled a second finger. "Two, I turn into a dragon, and we fly." A smile threatened to appear as he explained, "So I'll be naked again." He decided her flushed scarlet cheeks were confirmation that she found him at least a little attractive. He raised a third finger. "Or three, you let me carry you. We still fly, but I stay dressed."

"What do you mean, carry me?"

"The same way I got you to the cave the night with the wolves. You were unconscious, so you don't remember." Stepping closer, he let his mischievous side take flight. He was grateful Raelyn didn't yet know him well enough to recognize the peculiar flick of his tail that constantly gave away that he was planning a prank on the others. "But it went something like this." He bent down and swooped her up, cradling her against his chest, and hoped she wouldn't hit him for his impertinence.

"What are you doing?" Raelyn yelped.

"Sweeping you off your feet and carrying you." He grinned down at her, judging by her glower that she'd caught his pointed reference to her confessed daydream of being swept off her feet by a shepherd boy. "So," he said, not bothering to hide his amusement. "Walking, dragon, or carrying?"

"You seem to have already decided."

"So you're saying you agree with me? Excellent." He unfurled his wings and soared upward before she had a chance to disagree—or Meredith or someone could happen upon them and ask any troublesome questions.

With a screech that made his ears ring, the princess hugged her arms around his neck. He could feel her heart racing as she pressed into his chest. Well, scaring her hadn't been his intention, but her dramatics amused him, and her clinging wasn't unwelcome. Unfortunately, though, some part of her arm was pressing against his throat, which wasn't pleasant.

"I'm not going to drop you, Princess," Alexander murmured close to her ear, fighting a smirk. "You don't have to strangle me."

"Sorry." The pressure on his windpipe eased, but she continued to cling to him. "It's your fault. You could have warned me!"

He smiled. "Where's the fun in that?"

"Oh, so it's fun to scare me to death? Is that it?" There was some genuine irritation in her tone, but also a hint of melodramatic teasing that reminded him of Lucas. If they both made it back to the cave after this trip and she didn't hate him, it gave him hope that they could truly become friends…but that was an uncomfortably big if.

"All right, I'm sorry," he said, hoping as he picked up speed that the wind didn't obscure his words. "Forgive me?"

"I'll think about it." Her grip on him relaxed further, and he could feel her breathing and heart rate had slowed.

Stars filled the sky like glittering rubies around a slender crescent moon that looked like it was blushing as it watched Alex carry Raelyn through the sky. It was only the red tint of his dragon vision compensating for the darkness so he wouldn't fly into trees, but the thought of a blushing moon amused him all the same.

Too soon, he caught the ashy scent of wood smoke and aroma of cooking venison. His jovial spirit fell away as they drew closer to Raelyn's family—and a contingent of very armed knights. A new fear that should have occurred to him sooner weighed down on him. What if the dragon felt threatened and he couldn't control it? He'd been so worried about Princess Raelyn's family hurting him, but what if he hurt them? Stubborn, pretty girls were an awful lot of trouble.

"Are you getting tired?" Raelyn asked.

"My arms are a touch stiff." It wasn't untrue, although it wasn't the reason for his sudden discomfort. "Don't worry, you're light," he added, keeping his tone untroubled with effort. "Besides, we're getting close. I smell smoke."

20

When the scent of human joined the smoke, Alex flew lower, moving slowly between the treetops as he caught glimpses of the Eynlaean campfires. Once he dared fly no closer, he landed on a barren section of the pass and carefully set the princess down—but he must not have been as gentle as he'd thought, because Raelyn wobbled, and her palm splayed against his chest as she steadied herself.

Alex stopped breathing, aware of nothing besides the pressure of her hand on his chest and her hair inches from his face. But as quickly as it happened, she straightened, and her hand left his shirt.

The sounds of a camp, of conversations around snapping fires and the metallic bangs and rustle of canvas tents, were unnervingly close.

Letting his dragon sight dim, since it seemed to unnerve her, Alex met Princess Raelyn's eyes and reminded her of their agreement. "We keep to the trees. Stay in shadow. You can look, but don't speak."

"I understand," she whispered.

That was the best he could expect. If she didn't keep her word… He'd just have to hope he was right to trust her. In an effort to remind her of that trust, he led the way into the forest, allowing her to follow. He hoped no one would hear the subdued rustle of her skirt against the ground or the occasional snap of a twig under Raelyn's feet over the noise of the camp.

Laughter carried through the trees. It seemed the Eynlaean retinue was relieved to be leaving the mountains in the morning. Alex doubted Prince Gareth would share their high spirits.

Once they were close enough to see individual Eynlaeans, Alex slipped back and placed a hand on Raelyn's shoulder so he could silently guide her into a crouch. She didn't flinch or lean away from him, merely looked over at him, waiting, like she really did plan on keeping her word. He put a finger to his lips before continuing forward, staying crouched and directing her with a gentle pressure on her shoulder while he watched the camp.

His gaze caught on King Weston, sitting by a fire next to a middle-aged woman with rigidly straight posture and golden hair who had to be Queen Margaret. Alex ushered Raelyn closer and brought them to a stop behind a bush between two pines. Hopefully the cover would be sufficient to shield them from wandering eyes while still allowing Raelyn to see her parents. Gareth wasn't around, and Alex hoped the prince wasn't roaming the forest. If the prince stumbled across them… A vision of Gareth grabbing Alex's horns and ripping him away from Raelyn flashed through his mind. With a breath to steady his nerves, Alex positioned himself at Raelyn's back and gripped both of her shoulders, just to provide a gentle reminder to stay quiet.

The princess pushed some branches out of her way, then clamped her hand over her mouth. A small tremor ran through her, but she didn't make a sound. Where was her brother? They couldn't afford to wait long, but Alex couldn't bear the thought of drawing Raelyn away before she got to see the brother she cared about so deeply.

The relief Alex felt when Gareth emerged from a tent near the Eynlaean king and queen was short lived. The prince ignored his father's call and strode directly toward Alex and Raelyn's hiding spot. Alex tensed, his fingers tightening on Raelyn's shoulders. The princess's breath hitched. Panic clawed at Alex's insides. This had been a mistake. Gareth was too close now, and if Raelyn screamed, Gareth would be upon them in an instant. Alex would be unable to escape without being seen, and Raelyn would go to Henry and Tristan while Alex would return to the cave fearing for his life and the safety of his friends—if he was able to get away at all. Images of being beaten and mocked as a monster while someone sawed off his wings before they bound him and delivered him to Henry stirred dragon fire in his chest.

Alex dragged Raelyn down lower behind the bush. The lavender of Meredith's soap wafted faintly from her hair. He closed his eyes, thinking of Meredith and the others, of his desire to not hurt or scare Raelyn again, and forced the dragon to sleep.

"You promised," he breathed into Raelyn's ear, his eyes still pressed closed as he worked to calm his fears.

He didn't see her nod, but he felt the movement as her hair brushed against his cheek. She either feared or trusted him enough not to break her promise, and in that moment, the reason didn't really matter.

Alex slowly opened his eyes, nearly panicking again when he spied Prince Gareth standing a few paces from where they knelt.

"I'll come back," Gareth whispered, his back slouched. "I'll find you. I know you're not dead." He craned his head back to look at the stars, heartbreak etched into his face. "I'd know. I'd feel it. As soon as I can get away, I'll come find you, Rae. Something took you, and I'll rescue you." A miserable smile pulled at his mouth as he kicked the ground. "Unless you kill the monster first. Right, Raelyn?"

Was that something the siblings had talked about? Killing monsters? Alex's thoughts darted back to Raelyn's threatening grip on the steak knife.

"Gareth!" Queen Margaret called. "Come back. Please stay close!"

Gareth huffed. "If I'm right"—the ice in his tone chilled even Alex's dragon-fire-infused blood—"whatever took you better hope you kill it before I find it." He stomped to his tent without acknowledging his parents in a petulant display that made Alex pity the poor king and queen.

Raelyn trembled, and Alex decided they needed to leave before Raelyn's resolve crumbled. Or before she started crying and accidentally drew attention.

He moved to a partial crouch. Raelyn didn't stir. He had to take Raelyn's hand and drag her up before she budged. She let him lead her through the forest, her eyes unfocused, and making so much noise Alex's heart was pounding. Back on the empty pass, he picked her up and unfurled his wings. He almost expected her to resist, or perhaps just hang limply in his arms, she seemed so dazed, but instead, she tucked her arms around his neck and rested her head against his chest.

In other circumstances, he might have been relishing the moment, but as they soared back up the mountains, a wetness spread on his torso. Her strangled sobs, muffled by the wind and her face pressing into his shirt, tore at his heart. He held her as tightly as he dared, trying to offer some measure of comfort, and flew more slowly to give her time to grieve before they landed and he'd have to face her.

The dark mouth of the cave came into view, and Alex eased to the ground. After he set Raelyn down, she simply stood there, so he took a step back to give her space. She didn't even look his way.

Alex hung his head and stared at the grass in the dim moonlight as chill night air brushed against his shirt, still damp with Raelyn's tears. "You must think me heartless," he whispered.

An amused snort drew his attention back up to the princess,

who had turned to face him and was watching him with an odd expression. She didn't appear angry—almost like she was laughing at him, as if what he'd said was funny. Maybe because she thought it was obvious that he was heartless?

"Sorry." Raelyn smiled. "You just…reminded me of a puppy."

His confusion multiplied. "A puppy?"

"You know, a baby dog. Little, furry, cute—"

"I've seen a puppy," Alex said with a roll of his eyes. Great, Raelyn could join his friends in teasing him about his guilty puppy look. Accursed tail. "But I'm not a baby, a dog, little, furry, or cute."

Her eyes danced above a teasing smirk. "Maybe, but you ducked your head and tucked your tail like a puppy."

"I'm not a puppy." He folded his arms over his chest as he tried to understand her shift in mood. Was she merely hiding her pain under the teasing, and beneath the smile, she hated him? Was this some new lie? "What are you doing?"

"What?" Raelyn messed with her skirt, her smile fading.

"I expected you to…yell at me," he said honestly. "Storm off. Refuse to speak to me. Something." Possibly try to kill him, but he didn't voice that out loud. "I didn't expect…whatever this teasing is." He sighed, almost afraid to ask for the truth, but he wouldn't be able to sleep if he didn't know. "Did that help at all? Or are you avoiding it because you hate me more now?"

Raelyn's mouth pinched as she appeared to consider while Alex grew increasingly anxious.

At last, she said, "It hurt. I'm angry my family thinks I'm dead. But I would've had to say goodbye to them, anyway. And Gareth wasn't happy about me marrying Tristan. If they didn't get along, he still would have been furious to leave me behind. It would be different, but it was always going to be hard for both of us. It breaks my heart to see him like that. Mourning and enraged."

That made sense and didn't seem very spiteful, but Gareth's threat was still ringing in his ears. Hesitantly, he asked, "Will you try to kill me?"

Raelyn's eyes widened. "No!"

"It's unlikely"—the words tumbled out before he had time to think better of them—"but if your brother found us…would you let him kill me? Maybe worse? It sounded like he would rip my wings off my back if he knew I had you and was given the chance." His vision flashed crimson as his tangled emotions heightened.

"Stop."

Alex barely heard her, his thoughts rushing in all directions—his own family's safety, King Weston's impossible choices, Raelyn's sorrow, his own growing affection for the princess, Henry's viciousness, Gareth's rage. "I don't know if I blame him. Should I have let you go? Should I have left you with them?"

His breaths came faster, and heat built in his chest. The dragon looking for a threat, but there was nothing to fight but his own choices and their consequences. Maybe Lucas and Jasper were wrong, and he wasn't wise enough to be a king, assuming he ever did get free of Henry's curse. He clutched the sides of his head as his tongue seemed to develop a mind of its own.

"You would have married my cousin if that manticore hadn't attacked. I never would have known. But I do know I can't send you into what might be a trap, I can't…" He roared to vent some of his frustration—at himself, at Henry, and at this curse that ruined his own life and, it seemed, the lives of the people he cared about.

"Alexander?"

The gentleness in her tone broke through his panic, and Alex jerked his gaze up to Raelyn, waiting like a parched man hoping for water.

"I don't want to marry Tristan. Not if everything you said is true."

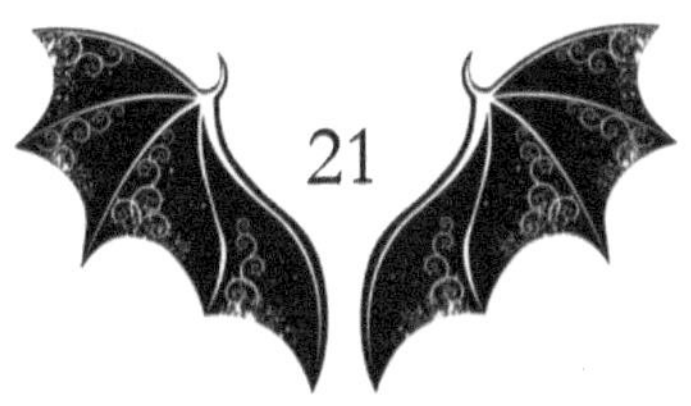

21

More than anything Princess Raelyn had done so far—asking him about his past, laughing with his family, keeping her promise at the Eynlaean camp, clinging to him while he flew—the words *I don't want to marry Tristan* gave Alex hope that she truly was starting to trust him. After how adamant she had been about her duty, only believing him could have changed her mind.

"I don't want to stay here, either," she said, and some of his happiness dimmed. "But if I go back to my family, I'll have to marry him. I'd have to call your uncle king and father while knowing what he did to you. I'd be required to give a murderer grandchildren while fearing he could turn on me any moment."

Alex barely suppressed a growl at the abhorrent idea.

"If I stay here, the Carbreys will believe I'm dead. Hopefully you're right, and they can't break a treaty over a dead princess. It's not my parents' fault if I'm dead." She wrapped her arms over her stomach, looking scared and vulnerable. "My father is smart and a good negotiator. He'll convince K…Henry to keep the treaty, even without the marriage."

"What will you do if you stay?" His face heated a little as he confessed, "I haven't given this any long-term thought."

Raelyn frowned. "I don't know. Wait until Tristan is married to someone else and then go home? I guess I don't need to decide tonight."

The thought of her leaving brought an unwarranted surge of disappointment, but Alex decided to embrace their progress and the possibilities inherent in forestalling any decisions.

"Can we go inside?" she asked, a hint of pleading in her voice as she shivered.

Alex blinked. He'd noticed the cold, but his dragon heat had compensated, and he mentally kicked himself for not considering Raelyn didn't have the same advantage. "Oh, right, sorry. Dragon blood. I rarely get cold."

Raelyn's brow furrowed. "Then why the blazing fire in the dining cavern?"

The… Alex fought a chuckle. "Dining cavern?"

"Well, it's not exactly a traditional hall or room."

"I like that. Dining cavern." Alex nodded, deciding from henceforth, everyone was absolutely calling it a dining cavern. Maybe manners weren't required in *caverns*. "And I might not get cold, but I like the heat."

As they walked side by side toward the cave, his mind abruptly caught up to something. The princess…had called him Alexander, the first time she had done so without his prompting.

My name isn't Princess, she'd told him. He gathered his courage. Such a simple thing, a name, and yet, it could mean so much.

"Raelyn."

"Yes?"

"Nothing." He smiled softly. "I just wanted to say your name. I like it. Raelyn. You said my name," he added, hoping she didn't think him too strange.

Raelyn shrugged, but there was something self-conscious about the movement. "How else am I supposed to address you? You there?" Alex nearly laughed, but Raelyn continued, "You said you wanted to be on a first-name basis, Alexander."

Who knew hearing a beautiful princess say his name could do such strange things to his heart? It was like being wrapped in an impossibly soft blanket, sitting in front of a fire, and sipping tea.

"Did you just…purr?"

"What?" He jerked to a stop in the cave entrance, heat flaming over his cheeks. Surely he hadn't. Had he? Lucas insisted Alex purred sometimes, but Alex never noticed—but then, he rarely noticed the embarrassing things his tail did. "I'm not a puppy, and I'm not a cat, either."

"You're blushing."

"I didn't purr," he protested, rankling at the indignity of the possibility his body could betray him like that. It would be so much worse than snoring.

"If you say so," Raelyn replied, moonlight playing across her teasing expression.

"I do." A slight snarl accompanied the words, which was em-barrassing enough on its own, but then Raelyn laughed. At least she didn't find the growling intimidating anymore…but laughing at him wasn't ideal, either.

Alex stomped over to the nook in the side of the cave where they kept torches handy and lit one before turning back to her. "I do not purr. That's ridiculous."

Raelyn's mouth twitched. "Of course."

With a huff, he led the way through the tunnels to Lucas's old room. They'd have to get started on outfitting a new one for him before the lad drove Jasper to insanity. The thought of Lucas's an-tics and the reminder that Raelyn was staying—and willingly, with potential to become a friend, if not more, took his mind off the mortification of Raelyn's purring accusations.

Raelyn opened the door on a dark, cold room. Alex handed her the torch and brushed past, headed for the fireplace. "I can get the fire going."

Thankfully, one of the others had already cleaned and prepared the fireplace, and all Alex had to do was breathe some fire onto the neatly stacked logs. The wood ignited, brightening the space and starting to fight the cold that always seem to cling to the stone walls, and Alex straightened. Raelyn handed him back the torch. He didn't need it, but it seemed awkward to say that, so he just accepted it.

"Goodnight, Raelyn."

A gentle smile bloomed on her face as she peered up at him through her blonde lashes, standing so close he could have leaned forward and kissed her forehead. "Goodnight, Alexander."

Maybe it was her intimate whisper, or the way she was looking at him, or her nearness, or perhaps it was merely the pleasant warmth of the fire at his back, but Alex felt his entire body relax, his muscles releasing all the stress of the day as if he'd just sunk into a hot bath.

Raelyn's eyes crinkled, and she laughed, shattering the moment. "What?"

"Nothing." She shook her head. "I just... I can't believe how terrified I was of a glorified, scaly cat."

Oh, not this again. "I didn't purr!" he insisted, the dragon glowering at being likened to a tiny mouse-catcher. Raelyn grinned, and he spun toward the door, his irritation growing as the cave took on a telltale scarlet hue. He took a calming breath, and the stone returned to a dark gray. "You're being rude."

"What's so much worse about purring than growling?"

He eyed her over his shoulder. "Purring is not princely or manly. Or even dragon-ly." It simply wasn't a respectable, attractive thing to do, but worse, it probably shouted *I have a crush on you.* As if he didn't have enough to overcome with the horns and claws and tail and wings and growling and breathing smoke, he could add *purring that reminds her of a pet* to the list of reasons Raelyn wouldn't ever return his nascent feelings of romance.

"I think it's adorable," she said matter-of-factly.

"Ador…" Not only a pet, but a cute, cuddly pet. Excellent. He snorted a bit of smoke. "Isn't there a happy medium somewhere between horrifying and adorable?"

"Like what?"

Alex fluffed the hair between his horns. "I don't know. Charming? Handsome?" Oh, great heavens, he'd said that out loud. "Nice?"

"Nice?"

He supposed nice didn't quite make sense as a halfway point between scary and cute. "I don't know. I'm tired." And clearly needed to get out of there before he said or did something any more ridiculous. He stepped into the tunnel and grabbed the door handle, but Raelyn caught the edge of the door, preventing him from closing it. He looked at her, confused.

"Back at the camp…" Raelyn rubbed her sleeve. "What would you have done if I broke my promise?"

The memory of his panic slid like ice down his spine. He let the fear go, reminding himself it was in the past. "I'm not sure. Covered your mouth and held you back, I guess. I'm unsure what else I could've done. Because I wouldn't hurt you or your brother." He hesitated a moment before admitting, "Honestly, I was terrified he was going to spot us."

She met his gaze, her face pinching. "You…were terrified?"

Did she think he didn't feel fear? Probably for the best to dissuade her of that idea, but all the same, Alex couldn't look at her as he admitted the truth. "If he had seen us, I would have had to choose whether to take you away, knowing he would hunt me, or let you go and hope he wouldn't come after me or tell anyone. I've been hiding for twelve years, and not just from my uncle. People like to kill things that scare them. Things they don't understand." He tried to lighten the moment with a smile and a poor joke. "Sometimes they wield steak knives."

His words seemed to have the opposite effect as Raelyn blanched. "Oh. I…I'm sorry." Her head drooped, and Alex had to fight the urge to lift his hand from the door handle and stroke her hair like he had after the manticore attack.

Something warm and soft touched his hand, and he started, looking down to see Raelyn's small, pale hand resting on top of his on the handle.

"I'm sorry," Raelyn said. "About all of it."

The connection was weaker through her hand than it would have been on her neck, but the skin-to-skin contact combined with the depth of her sincerity was enough for the dragon to know—Raelyn wasn't lying.

His heart racing, Alex looked from their hands up to Raelyn's sapphire eyes reflecting the light of his torch. He opened his mouth, but words failed him. Before he could start purring again—not that he ever had in the first place—he gulped, forced out a hasty "goodnight," and hurried away.

After Alex snuffed out the torch and returned it to the mouth of the cave, he went to his room, thankful to find it unoccupied. He got his own fire going and pulled off his boots. Flopping onto his stomach on his bed, he let out a contented sigh. Tomorrow would mark the first day of a new normal in the cave. A new life where Raelyn was there, where he would do his best to protect her the same way he did the rest of his family. Maybe he couldn't reunite her with her family while the treaty calling for her marriage to Tristan existed, but he would strive every day to make her feel like a part of his family and look for ways to draw out her heart-stopping smile and laughter. His nose wrinkled.

Other than purring. Although…on second thought, maybe *ador-able* wasn't as bad as he feared. Adorable to attractive seemed an easier transition than repulsive to attractive. As long as he didn't purr in front of the others. They'd never let him hear the end of it.

But he could figure that out later. For now, Alex would relish knowing that Raelyn trusted him and no longer feared him. The comfortable heat of the fire and the thought of Raelyn's whispered *goodnight, Alexander* lulled him to sleep, and he dreamt of blue eyes and gold-touched hair and flights under the stars with a stubborn yet kind princess in his arms.

Also Available

About *Prince of Shadow and Ash*:

She could be his light…if his darkness doesn't destroy them.

Bastard and former mercenary Lord Regulus Hargreaves' resolve is crumbling. He's desperate to pay off his debt to the sorcerer who enslaved him, but after two years, he fears he'll never be free of the cursed mark that won't even let him die. Then Lady Adelaide sees past his scar and shadowed past, and Regulus' dying hope rekindles.

But will loving Adelaide while serving the Prince of Shadow and Ash put her in danger?

Adelaide Belanger yearns to use the magical energy within her, but revealing her power could get her killed--like every other mage in the kingdom. When she meets kind and rugged Regulus, she wonders if she has finally found someone to trust with her secret— and her heart. Regulus and Adelaide struggle to protect their romance and keep their secrets from predatory nobles and the devious sorcerer.

By the time their secrets are revealed, it may be too late for them both...and possibly for the entire kingdom.

About the Author

Selina R. Gonzalez is a Colorado native with mountains in her blood and dreams that top 14,000 feet. She loves chocolate, fantasy, costumes, bread, history, superheroes, faux leather, things that sparkle, medieval Britain, snark, dogs, and Jesus—not in that order.

She loves to travel and has driven coast-to-coast in the US, visited Britain three times, and has a list of places to go as long as Pikes Peak is tall, but always comes back home to Colorado.

You can find Selina raving about books she's enjoying (or adding to her bottomless pit of a to-be-read pile) on Facebook at Selina R. Gonzalez, Author and on Instagram at @NightTooIsBeautiful, and being generally goofy and snarky as well as talking about writing, life, and the antics of her family's dogs in her IG stories. Make sure you don't miss any of Selina's future books by subscribing to her newsletter at:

SelinaRGonzalez.com/newsletter-subscription/